ONE VOICE

CRYSTAL WHITE

PAGE PUBLISHING, INC.
New York, NY

First originally published by Page Publishing, Inc. 2019

ISBN 978-1-64544-226-4 (Paperback)
ISBN 978-1-64544-227-1 (Digital)

Printed in the United States of America

Past, Present, Future

My *love* continues to be enriched through the *years*.

My dearest sons, Taylor and Shane.

My *heart beats* with my passed husband, Shawn.

My *soul mate*, Daniel. Daniel and I are walking the path together. He is my brightest *star*.

Mariah—beautiful friend, daughter of *hearts*.

Sister of hearts, kindness, and friendship—my sisters of hearts, Kimmie, Darla, Laura, and Katie.

Family does not have to be linked in blood. A true *family* bond is with unconditional *love*.

Aces of Hearts, Frank Vern.

Queen of Hearts, Mother Loyce Cossitt.

CONTENTS

Chapter One

ONE VOICE

The hardest thing I ever have done in my fifty-three years of breathing is writing my story.

It is not a happy story at the beginning, but it does have a beautiful ending, wonderful, aspiring middle. The ending is still being created.

I want more than anything for my words to inspire, influence and create a vibrant painting of survival. It is a pilgrimage from memories.

Time, space, and balancing the facts, while maintaining control of my emotions, this became difficult because I would feel the past seeping into my emotions. I found myself in a dark, evil depression. Memories flooded through the center of my universe. No place was safe in brain; my world was insane. Overwhelming sadness.

While I was writing, I realized the emotions draining. Chaos appeared. Scars stained my body, heart, and mind. *No peace.*

My mind was rewinding the emotions with the evilness from a parent, a parent who was to protect, keep you safe, and love with unconditional ties.

In my case, the parent was the one who created my *hell*. The battle scars from my childhood, teenage, and early youth became the war zone.

I know, without a doubt, I required assistance. My sanity was torn from my mind. I was no longer able to separate emotions from facts. The terror and the nightmares rubbed throughout my entire body. I was no longer safe. My inner peace was invaded by the evilness, hatred, and darkness. I could no longer fight alone. I am warrior, yet I still needed my *Lord Jesus Christ* to protect and shield me from the demon that dwelled in my past.

I was no longer able to close the mind from the horror and torment from mother and my brothers.

I was questioning the purpose of my existence: what, why, and who.

I challenged every second, truth, and reasoning.

I located the perfect therapy, life coach. This journey is long and extremely difficult by myself.

I learned that I am my own person. I am telling a story, but that does not mean I have to be emotional, to relive the nightmare. The past should and will not define me in the future. Only I can conquer my demons. I needed spiritual guidance.

The past does not define the future. I needed to make amends to my inner child. The girl who became abused and forgotten—she needed a voice. She needed to be heard, to be unchallenged about the abuse.

Yes, faith is a strong witness and instructor. My teacher was the *beginning* and the *end* of man's life. *God is the word, Omaga* and *Alpha*.

I had to see myself as a worthy, honorable, and respected woman. I am a decent person. I truly needed to believe in myself, to *love* myself.

I deserve true love, to love without expectations, no contract, no strings attached to my heart.

I am a *Christian*. I am *beautiful*. I am *me*.

I needed to surround myself with positive, caring, and loving people, guard myself from evil, sadness, and negative souls.

I put my trust in *God*. He proved to me that there is a place for a broken spirit. *God* guided me into loving arms. I felt joy and happiness for the first time in my life.

I heard encouraging words. I was given a brand-new structure to build my life with. I was given the chance to feel true *love*. I was given a better and happy life, a life that *God* has given and will give to those who trust and love him.

Unfortunately, not every person who has endured *abuse* survives. *Suicide* has become their only source of *peace*. To conquer their terrible life seems untouchable. Demons lurked in every aspect of their lives.

I did have a dark world in my childhood. I did not see a silver lining in my future. I only felt, saw, and heard *death*.

Death was filled with *demons*, waiting for the chance to push me into that dark, lonely, and evil *hell*.

Demons wanted my *soul*, my *heart*, my *mind*.

I fought the battle, and I still *am*.

Looking inside myself, I tried to find value in my whole makeup as a human being, a woman, a mother, a wife, a friend, and an employee.

I needed to acknowledge that I was important. I was valuable. I was worthy.

I needed to put my family at the top of priority list.

I placed my career first, then my family, and last, *God.*

I *changed* the priority list: first, *God*; second, myself; third, family; and fourth, career.

My work environment was toxic to my health. I would cover shifts if someone called off work. I would answer my beeper on my days off. I would not travel a long distance from my job in case there was an emergency.

Was I thanked for my dedication to my job? Was I given hand on the back for doing an outstanding job?

The answer is no.

Was I being targeted due to my *illness*?

The answer is yes.

I learned to write down almost everything I said or did in my *job.*

This illness had caused many problems.

I did not always remember what tasks or questions that I would be required to do. I would carefully orchestrate my words into sentences and answer questions with follow-up answers. Therefore, I could answer clearly without prejudice in my answers. My mind was not able to remember as well as it used to. There were days that I believed that I was going *crazy.* I would walk from one room to another, and in a short distance, I forgot what I was getting and why.

If I was approached from someone about my habits of sticky notes, or repeating the question, I would smile with a gesture of wanting to be wonderful to the clients and their personal needs. Always giving a smile and handshake, I sometimes would explain that I had a senior moment for not retrieving the requested item.

I was a shattered brain. There was no *doubt.*

Am I glad I am alive?

Some days I would answer, *yes.*

Other days, my answer was *no*.

I questioned *God*, why am I here? What is my purpose? Why do I have a voice?

Guess what? I do have a purpose.

I am able to speak for other abused children, teenagers, and adults.

I will speak for the persons who cannot utter a word due to fear.

I will shine the light upon a person who is afraid of the dark.

I will hold and encourage an abused person, giving them strength

Abuse does not belong in a dark, hidden closet. It should not be a secret. Abuse is, and should be, treated like a cruel, ugly, and dark spoken forum.

All it takes is one loud voice! The abuser deserves to be shown in the light, no longer hiding in the shadows of the darkness.

Watch out! My voice is loud and demands to be heard!

If an abuser thinks they can hide, think again!

My life has a purpose.

The abused person has a purpose.

Soon the demons will have no place to hide!

Funny how my past has brought me full circle. With no past, I have no future. Without memories, I have no goals. With no experiences, there is no endurance. Your past is the insight. What I do not want and sometimes what I gained is wisdom.

Some people say I am a survivor. No, I am not. I carry the burden of my abusers.

Some people say I am a *hero*. No, I am not. I am God's child. I do not want praise. I do not want tears. I do not want to continue reliving the cruelty.

I want a voice. I want to be heard. I want to be understood. I did not ask to be born. I am here, and I will live my life to the fullest.

After seventeen years of being tormented by my *abusers*, I took back the power. My destiny belongs to me.

My past will never define *me*.

Without tools to direct my decisions, I have made mistakes.

I have not failed as long as I learned from my experiences.

I accomplished a few goals. I have many more to challenge myself:

1. Love my children.
2. Protect my children.
3. Stand my ground; no one will hurt my children. No scars, no bad memories. My children will find purpose.
4. Respect my children. Respect my husband. Respect myself.
5. God, Jesus Christ, Holy Spirit will always be at the top of my list. God, Jesus Christ, and Holy Spirit. Me—I need to take care of myself; otherwise, I am not able to care for children. Until they become eighteen, they are my concern. Husband—he will be moved into third place after the children reach eighteen years of age.
6. Children are a loan from God. Children are gifts and blessings.

On my tombstone, I would like it to read:

Crystal, a daughter of our Lord.
A beloved wife who loved with all her being.
A mother; each day was a blessing to love and comfort her sons.
A grandmother; her heart runneth over with pride.

My day with my beloved Lord is my reward for loving, honoring, and having loyalty to all those I treasured.

I do not know what my purpose will be here on *earth*.

I tried more than twice to end my life. God sent an angel to protect me with his wings. My Angel, Mikheal, stood between me and death.

I would like to explain my destiny with Mikheal.

My life would not be complete without my *faith*.

Faith was the strength that gave me *peace*, the determination to conquer my demons from the *past*: rebellion, stubbornness, and self-preservation.

I believe God created a safety net within the brain.

The brain has a rewind and play buttons, not a delete. When memories are so horrific, the brain will store the details. Until you are able and prepared to watch the memories, it remains stored. Like watching a black-and-white film, characters are portrayed with slow movements. Cruel and unimaginable scenes are beyond graphic words. Masks being torn off faces, and the identity is revealed.

I saw the masks. I saw faces. *Evil*, dark, and blazing red eyes—*devil*.

Frightening snarls of their souls. Their words covered with secrets. Secrets carved into memories. The body was torn and shattered like broken glass.

My memories unraveled with all sides busting at the seams.

I stored my secret memories with a huge pink bow. The memories were carefully placed in a box inside my mind. The memories began to shred throughout my mind. Suddenly memories flooded my mind.

Little by little, each memory had a story to reveal: scenes from abuse throughout my childhood. As the memories trickled, each nerve became a stream of words and actions.

My heart was hallowed, stripped from emotions.

As adults who survived childhood trauma, the abused had a voice.

My voice had secrets to tell. These secrets were not my secrets. The secrets belonged to *cowards*, hiding behind a mask in the darkness

Why? Why did I keep their secrets for so long?

These were not my secrets to keep anymore!

I was programmed to keep secrets. As young children, we are in consent fear of the *abuser*.

Maintaining a normal life—*How* is this possible?

You keep the secrets inside your mind, heart, and soul.

I remained silent.

I was instructed to remain hidden, not be heard, and always keep the secret. Admit nothing. I was to blame for my *abusers'* actions. It was my fault. I carried the blame, the shame.

I was taught no one would believe me. I would be accused of lying.

I decided I would no longer remain *silent*. My voice will be *loud*. I will be *heard*.

One voice can make a difference.

My strength, I will shoulder others who are *abused*. I will be Their *voice*.

I have *wisdom*.

I am *worthy*.

I will not remain in the background.

I will protect the children.

I am no longer a *victim*.

I am extremely proud of my *accomplishments*.

I am not afraid of the dark. My nightmares were no longer my *burden*.

I will and can relive the terrible memories. If I can *help* one *child*, it is worth the *pain*.

I am worth millions of *tears*.

I am worthy to have *happiness* and *joy*.

I will hold out my hand, gather the children *abused*, and comfort them.

I will keep my *promise*.

To my *abusers, hell*—it is here. I will not hold your secrets. My memories, they are your jailer, your judge, and your prison.

There is no safe place to hide.

You will remember my name.

No place is safe.

Your sleep will be tormented with all your victim's names, their faces, and your mind will find no peace.

Every waking hour you will see only the faces of your victims. There will be no sanctuary *because* I am *here*.

Emotional Damage

As a wife, mother, and working woman having a career outside the home, I managed to push through secret tormenting emotions—

Emotions that I managed to place inside an invisible box. This box held all the dark secrets wrapped with a pretty pink bow. By placing these emotions away, I could move forward, hopefully upward, mostly upward.

I tried desperately to *push* through my hideous childhood drama.

Fortunately, my brain would allow certain amount of memories flood through my mind. Dark, ugly, and sadness crept silently in my dreams and waking hours. A smell, sound, voice or situation would trigger these memories.

I do not have a computer chip in my brain. I am not able to delete, or reboot memories. There is not a doubt that *God* has placed a security system in my brain, allowing trickles of memories out of my pretty pink bowed box little at a time. Memories to acknowledge, and deal with the abuse. I kept hidden in my box of secrets. One step at a time.

Sometimes, without warning, I would recall a situation that bled into my subconscious mind. It was like viewing a black-and-white film. But this film was authentic with sound. Very *real*. I had no control or the ability to stop the projector. The cruel and dark scenes played each moment clearly.

My world was *hell*. The emotions of *hate, anger,* and *disdain* painted a portrait of my childhood. It was a horror film.

The cataclysmic drama crept into my dreams. Trying to sleep without the nightmares became impossible. I would be awakened from a peaceful sleep, into an abyss of *demon hell*. Color black was the only color that I am able to describe with details of the covert cruelty that I endured throughout my childhood.

Waking up from my nightmare, the terror outlined from my sheets, with pillows soaked with my sweat and tears. I would try desperately to escape the horror, which engulfed every second I breathed. Sometimes I felt these memories would extinguish my life.

While awake, my mind would have visions of recurring memories I found no place to. hide. Muffling my screams with my hand, I would bite my hand so hard blood gushed through the open wound.

My reality was crying uncontrollably. Yet only dry tears appeared from my eyes. Wet tears no longer existed.

I lost count of how many times I woke from drenched covers, teared pillows, and pee lingering on my bedsheets from *fear*. The *fear* silenced my screams of *hatred*. Hearing footsteps echoing through my mind, I would try to stop breathing, try to stop my heartbeat.

The memory of each footstep paced with my heartbeats. The deep breaths of the *evil assaulted* from a shadow. The sour-smelling breath pushed my body into the mattress. The foul stench of the shadow's sweat, The only smell that remained upon my body from the assault, was the smell of stale alcohol spilling into my skin.

Brutality left my *heart, soul,* and *faith* marked with scars that were no longer seen on the body, and wounds tattooed each assault till there was no room left on my body to place more tattoos.

I heard every cuss word, every negative and cruel word known in the dictionary.

There are many terms and definitions that describe *abuse*.

The negative adjectives in the *English language*, The dictionary cannot describe the *pain* that words caused. The bruises were not seen on the body. Emotions of *hate* left the mind tormented from the *emotional abuse*.

Emotional and psychological *abuse*—there were no borders between the *abuser* and the *victim*. Environment and finances are not limited to one type of *person*.

Emotional abuse, physical abuse, and sexual abuse are usually placed upon young children. It is very easy to plant and formulate an image to groom a child with innocence. They trust and are unaware of the *evil abusers'* cruelty that has seeped onto their path.

Children are only an object, no longer seen as a human to the *abuser*. Children lose their innocence and trust, and through brain-washing, they lose their childhood.

Believe me, a child will take responsibility for the abuse. They learn and are told that the actions of an *abuser* was the child's fault. The *abuser* does not hold back any fear tactics upon the child. The *abuser* uses threats and guilt, and in a small amount of time, the *abuse* has become full circle.

Children want only to please and be loved. The *abuser* will use this emotion to their advantage, telling the child, *I love you.*

Giving gifts or just attention gain trust to the *abuser.*

When a child is told that they are not loved, if the child tells someone, this places *fear* into the child—fear of abandonment. Soon the child will show affection toward the *abuser. The child* does not have resentment toward the *abuser,* but follows instructions. The child wants love. If a child has a terrible home environment and is shown or given presents, they will perform like a puppet.

There is no *age, sex,* or finances that are prejudices to *abuse.*

My first memory of *abuse* occurred while I was still in a baby crib, not even two years of age.

Definitions of Three Assaults Are as Follows

Emotional and Psychological Abuse

A type of abuse that you experience in an abusive relationship. *Although it does not* leave an outward scar, it will leave a huge scar on your mind. Sometimes this can and will leave an invisible scar that creates a hardship in society and personal relationships. Your mind has triggers that impact your daily life: your confidence, how you see yourself, and self-image.

This is a silent abuse, yet it has a terrible impact on your thoughts. This does not always involve shouting or criticism. Emotional abuse can be silent and slow.

Also, it is usually under the radar: no witnesses, blending into the daily life, the background never truly noticed.

Emotional abuse or psychological mental abuse and the trigger to empower the abuser uses isolation, criticism, and maintaining low self-esteem on their victim. Some emotional abusers will say they are "teaching, correcting, and advising, even explaining" to the victim; and this way, the person who witnessed the situation will no longer question. Yet some outsiders who notice the actions of the abuser, a family member or friend, still question the behaviors of the abuser, and are told, "Mind your business." The abuser will maintain the righteous answers.

Physical Abuse

Physical abuse is any intentional act that causes injury or trauma a to another person, or animals, by the way of bodily contact.

Usually children, mentally ill, and handicapped become the target of becoming a victim.

Sexual Abuse

Sexual abuse means unwanted sexual activity. Perpetrators use force, make threats, or take advantage of victims unable to give consent. It is an act of having sex with a child, older adult-senior person, plus the disabled citizens; the infliction of sexual contact upon a person's compulsions.

There are so many levels, definitions, terms that describe *abuse*. Each abuse does leave scars. The hidden scars are from emotional abuse.

This abuse is invisible to the naked eye at first glance. You will notice the abuse clearly as you become familiar to the individual.

People react to directions and inner actions cautiously. The mannerisms are also noticeable.

Verbal Abuse

This also is a deep-rooted scar. The victim is screamed, yelled, at, put down, given no purpose in their well-being. This will start the beginning of lack of self-esteem. The root of self-doubt.

I personally felt that everything was and has been my fault. This was from the continued *yelling* and *screaming*, repeatedly told that I was at fault. If someone questioned or witnessed the actions of the abuser, I was at fault. Therefore, I received more beatings and insults.

I could or would not look directly into another person's eyes. I was instructed to keep my face lowered to the ground, never looking into the face of another. *No eye contact.*

This was considered a social skill, and I was not allowed to interact in social groups. I was carefully monitored at family gatherings or school functions. I dared not say or tried to participate in activities. I was to stay in the background and not be *seen*.

Behind closed doors, no one could or wanted to acknowledge the cruelty and battered victim. The attacker would and could continue the horror, nor did anyone try to intervene.

If a family member made a comment or gesture toward my well-being, I became the target of another beating, usually worse than before. If I was the cause of certain attention that was questioned by someone, and my abuser felt I needed to be dealt with immediately, it would be addressed. Taking me out of hearing range and visual sight, I would be taken to an isolated area. I would be hit with the belt on any part of my body; no part of my body was safe. After I was dealt with, I was then instructed to remain out of sight 'til it was time to leave. There was no rhyme or reason to the beatings. Sometimes the hand or foot would be used if there was no time to get a belt or branch from a tree. I learned to remain silent, out of sight. Whimpering from the welts and bruises upon bruises appeared.

Sexual Abuse

There are many levels of scars. I dared not to speak or approach in an adult about this secret activity. I was instructed and coached in my early years that no one would believe me. I would be put in foster care or put in children's jail. No one would believe a child over an adult's word. No one would save me from this disgusting person who was abusing me.

Even today as I write about this horrible subject, I still shake from terror. The sadness has cradled into my heart and mind. Who would believe me? I lived in a middle-class family. I looked like a normal girl. I spoke only when I was instructed from the abuser.

I relived this nightmare; every word I write brings a harsh feeling and anger toward the childhood abuser. I relived every kick, hit, and nasty word, to the backhanded slaps onto my body, soul, and mind.

I am taking back my sanity, and I am giving every symbol to each word purpose, every sexual encounter, every negative spoken word from this disgusting being to the light. They are no longer going to be able to hide in the dark. They do not deserve to be called human beings or animals because animals were better to their children than most.

I am *taking back my life, my happiness, my dreams.*

My dreams will no longer be nightmares. My dreams will be filled with a new beginning.

These are my words, *my abusers will find forgiveness.*

I will no longer carry a dark heart because they are not worth any more spilled tears, no more sadness, and the victory belongs to me.

I will not protect them.

My life will no longer be covered with a dark black veil of secrets. I deserve a pure *heart.* I deserve a wonderful life. I deserve a fulfilling life.

I will *no longer allow my past to define my future.*

I may be able to forgive, but I will not forget.

The power is *now mine.*

I take away their power to trespass into my thoughts, heart, and soul.

Hear no evil. Speak no evil. See no evil.

I asked myself this question over and over again, "Why did no one speak out about the horrors I endured?" The *abuse*—I continued to relive all through my childhood!

My relatives pretended not to hear the cruel, negative emotional and physical *abuse*! Relatives had deaf ears. "HEAR NO EVIL!"

Teachers did not report the physical bruises, the malnutrition on a skeleton body of a child: black eyes, dirty clothes, and unbathed child that sat in their classroom. "*Speak no evil.*"

Authorities did not see the emotional and physical evidence of terrible *abuse.*

"See no evil."

Enrolled in the *Park County School District, Cody, Wyoming,* I attended the kindergarten to second grade. No one spoke up! No one cared about a misfit girl.

Riverton, Wyoming, I attended third grade through fifth. No one spoke up about a girl with bruises, hungry, with homework not being turned in.

During class at each school, not only was I abused at home, but also at the cruel remarks from classmates. Sometimes teachers would talk to the students about their behavior. Usually, no one spoke up!

Teachers, school employees, and administration—no one spoke up!

School days, another place of hell!

I feel like an outcast!

I was the target of embarrassing, ridiculed jokes by students and teachers.

No one spoke up!

Once in a while, a teacher would give me extra attention. Give me a treat, like a snack, or just a smile. Kindness of a positive word was a godsend to a forgotten child.

I did not retaliate against the cruel injuries of smirking smiles or giggling hidden behind cupped hands of the whispering behind my back. I would encounter jeers and unkind words at recess and lunch periods.

No one spoke up!

I would place myself in isolation; staying out of sight was my way of survival, keep myself from individuality a secret. I longed for a refuge. Finding solitude under the school bleachers, my only triumph from harassment and snickers from other students was sometimes going to the nurse's office, giving me a place of isolation and a welcomed place to be secure.

No one spoke up!

No one saw an *abused child*!

Chapter Two

CIRCLE OF ABUSE

My mother, Shirley Ann Smith-Gorton-White, was born 1941, in Boise, Idaho, to an abusive family.

My grandmother, Doris Smith, was thirteen when she was forced into a marriage with Merton "Bud" Smith. My grandmother was pregnant with my mother.

The marriage was full of violence, cruelty, and a dominating man. My grandfather showed his cruel and emotional abuse toward my grandmother and my mother.

After the marriage dissolved between my grandparents, my mother endured worse abuse from my grandmother and several male friends that became extremely friendly to my mother. This would cause angry beatings and punishment from my grandmother (Doris).

My mother was born to a child-mother, who had no coping skills and very limited education.

During World War II, and also the post war, jobs were limited. This was a trigger toward my mother for beatings. My mother was not aware that a bottle of milk or clean diapers were not as important as the whiskey or gentlemen friends that swirled around the home.

My great-grandmother, Ada, tried to care for my mother, but the jealousy from my grandmother would result into welts, slaps, and cruel words to my mother. My great-grandmother (Ada) would try to shield my mother by keeping her close to her and hiding my mother in a closet when my grandmother (Doris) searched for my mother.

When my grandmother wanted to be a single woman without a child, she would drop my mother with other family members or strangers.

The result of these actions from my grandmother kept the circle or cycle of child abuse continuing through another generation.

My grandmother (Doris) seemed to be plagued by demons— the demons in the family tree. Each generation had been in chaos due to the lack of love, care, and morals.

The horrors and relentless beatings my mother endured from my grandmother (Doris) now became my *hell*. My mother gave endless beatings, insults, and never-ending badgering about my appearance.

I searched for explanations and reasons. *Why? How?* And *What?*

Why did this continue?

How do you stop the cycle of abuse?

What did these adult figures gain from harming, overpowering, and controlling innocent victims?

I have searched through the family tree, and I have come to the conclusion for their actions, which were either, Satan, Devil, or demons; bad blood running through the veins; or mental illness.

I believe that both my mother and grandmother had a severe mental disorder. Neither one could have empathy, affection, nor joy in their mental emotions.

Looking into my mother's eyes, I would see blackness in her heart, and her soul was even masked with darkness.

Both of these two women I was to pattern my life with or to. I changed the measurements, the pattern changed, and my existence was only by the hand of *God*.

I believe as young children, we have no control or power to be anyone but what our parents, or guardians instruct us to be.

As adults, *we change* the *pattern.*

We change the rule book.

Both mother figures in my childhood had no tenderness in their hearts. Usually, they were ambivalent in having difficulties in their choices with decisions. They would let their emotions, or lack of, affect their relationships. Family members were avoided if there were questions about the welfare of the child.

Most family and friends stayed away or kept their eyes shut.

The mood swings would change as fast as lightening, never really knowing which personality would surface. Anything or anyone could cause a cuss word, and then as soon as the mother inhaled, a fist would be slapped onto the child. No body parts were immune from beatings.

I walked on eggshells, trying to remain a shadow, be silent, and hide.

I believe both my mother and grandmother had multiple personality disorder, going from mild emotion to a severe rampage.

My mother would go into a rage, expecting someone to come to her aid, as if she was in distress. She would create a scene of being unjustly crucified. This would happen usually when she was questioned or accused of lying, stealing, or having affairs. My mother would explain her motives; poor me, and no one understands.

During one of her rages, my mother felt everyone was against her; her eyes turned dark black, and her face mashed into a frightening *demon*. I became extremely scared of her, and I would hide.

Somehow, she would find me, and of course, this made my mother even madder. Her yelling and slaps against any part of my body would be her target. Mother would scream that it was my fault, and she was treated like an outcast. She was not invited to parties at family functions. The holidays were the worst of all. My mother would call other family members, telling one person that another family member said this or that, which were lies. My mother craved the drama and being center of attention.

If I tried to talk to my mother and defend myself from mother's accusations, I just wish I would have learned to be quiet. Unfortunately, I did not ever achieve that asset.

There seems to be two themes that both of my mother and grandmother (Doris) had in common.

One common thread was victimization, appearing to encompass a huge spectrum, ranging from both women, maintaining and coaxing others to do things for them, or within extreme patterns of self-destruction to encourage and exploit using abusive mannerisms, either to themselves but mainly to defenseless persons.

Both women complained about feeling lonely and empty inside. They would also isolate and become distant from any contact with friend or family members. If someone had a bad health problem or problem in the family unit, my mother would comment that she was going through or had gone through the same issues, but my mother's health was worse than other persons.

There usually was no warmth and understanding from both my mother and grandmother (Doris). *No emotions!* Their lives were always in chao; no joy or happiness was allowed into their world.

Behavior patterns underlying the theme of victimization is best characterized as being incompetent and a contagiousness to others of their sense of emotional intensities.

Chapter Three

CIRCLE OR CYCLE OF CHILD ABUSE

The circle or cycle of child abuse continued throughout my family linage. I do have some knowledge of child abuse that was inflicted upon my mother from my grandparents.

My grandmother (Doris) kept the circle or cycle of abuse to the next generation.

I heard and read about the terrible incidents that my mother (Shirley) endured from my grandmother. The worst was during my mother's teenage years.

My mother was groomed, and she learned the same harshness and cruelty to torment her own children.

I vowed that I would end child abuse with *me!* I would not continue the cycle of emotional, sexual, and physical abuse upon my children. Nor would I allow anyone else to inflect any pain upon their souls. This included my husband (Shawn).

I listened to relatives discuss the terrible treatment that was beat upon my mother's body, the welts left on her legs, shoulders, and her back swollen from the impact from a tree branch or belt buckle. The scars that were left on my mother were not only physical, but emotional.

Yet *no one* spoke up. The silence that sealed my mother's fate is just as bad, as if these relatives placed the welts on my mother themselves.

I have the *power* and *control* to stop the cycle or circle of child abuse.

I have the insight to acknowledge the difference between discipline and abuse.

I have the *power*, and I have broken the chains of *abuse.*

I also have *faith.* I could, should, and would stop the pain from inflicting the *hate, sadness,* and *evilness* from my *heart* and *soul* for my children. My life is worth more than being another link in the chain of ABUSE.

My mother's story began with darkness. She was born to an army soldier and my grandmother (Doris). My grandmother became a mother at the tender age of thirteen. My grandfather (Merton "Bud" Smith) was threatened that if he did not marry Doris, my great-grandmother (Ada) would tell my grandfather's commander at the Army base of my grandfather's rape on my grandmother.

My grandparents had a small civil wedding at the courthouse.

If my grandfather committed this unthinkable sex act during my century, he would have been charged with RAPE on a minor. He would have been imprisoned. But in this time of *World War II* and *post war*, this subject was not a concern to the authorities.

My grandfather left his linage upon his daughters and grand-daughter. I believe that my grandmother was a victim of his wrath of hate. He was forced to marry my grandmother. My grandmother was a child bride.

Again, I state, a silent abuser is the bystander who is aware of the abuse, either by witnessing or hearing of the abuse, yet they say nothing. My grandfather, Merton Smith, got away with several acts of sexual deviant acts upon young girls. The age was not a factor. His sexual animal abuse was also placed upon me.

My mother, Shirley, never accused my grandfather of any abuse. But I would not say he didn't. His sexual abuse upon my aunt (Rosie) and myself is a record of his molestation. He molested the females in the family unit, He knew the correct threats to use and rewards to keep the daughter and granddaughter silent, to keep his SECRET!

Rosie was my aunt from my grandfather's third marriage.

Rosie did have the courage to tell her mother about the moles-tation and rape that was inflicted by her father, my grandfather.

Rosie explained in detail of the inappropriate touching and threats that she received from my grandfather.

I believed Rosie because I too was molested by the monster who called himself the teacher of *love-making*.

The family unit circled around my grandfather; the other sib-lings, including my mother, called Rosie a liar, that Rosie only wanted attention. She also wanted her mother and father to stay married. Rosie's attention to the sexual assault divided the family with her accusations.

My grandfather's threats were, "No one will believe you," and "It is your fault that I have to do this. You were pleading for the attention!"

My grandfather had the skills and dialogue. He groomed his victims to keep his disgusting secret. The secret also remained my secret until my grandfather's body was placed into the six-foot grave, which now has engulfed his secrets too.

In truth, it is my grandfather's secret *now*. No longer *mine*!

The cycle or circle of abuse continued onward and toward me by both my mother and family members.

I vow that the abuse ends with me!

By the time my mother was two years old, my grandmother had left my grandfather, and she was seeing other men. My mother was left with great-grandmother (Ada); this was only when my grandmother wanted to play the part of widow, and she had no children. My mother knew she was unwanted and a curse to my grandmother.

During the times my mother was left in the care of others, she was comforted by loving arms. But when my grandmother came back for my mother, the emotions that gripped my mother was terror, the overwhelming fear of my grandmother.

My mother would feel beatings, and this was an everyday punishment. Sometimes the men that grandmother brought home would also use a straight razor strap on my mother. My grandmother would enjoy the beatings and make jokes regarding the poor little girl.

There were days that when no one could care for my mother; she would be locked in a closet for days.

The feeling of terror always was the one emotion that remained with my mother through her childhood.

My aunt told me that one of our relatives witnessed the brutal abuse that my mother endured from my grandmother.

My mother was only a few weeks old. She was crying and disturbing my grandmother's sleep. My grandmother threw the infant into the wall.

My grandmother was unaware that my aunt saw this.

My aunt picked my mother up and soothed her cries. The aunt treated the incident to baby blues.

My mother grew up in fear, and she learned to hate my grandmother, as I have learned to despise my mother.

My mother and I have many things in common.

As children, we were both mentally and physically abused. We both grew into womanhood. *We* both wanted a better life.

However, my mother failed. She continued the cycle of child abuse to her children. My mother said to her sisters that she tried not to follow in her mother's footsteps. Also, she cannot retrace her steps and change the past, therefore, she needed to move forward.

My mother stated to her sister that she prayed that her children will forgive her for all things she did to them and the arguments that were made due to her neglect.

I am trying to release the darkness from my heart. It is not an easy task. The one person who was supposed to protect and care for children left a dark, deep, and brutal mark upon my body and my heart. My mother did not worry or care about the outcome of the attack she placed on her children.

So I asked myself, Why would she care if I forgive her?

I needed to forgive her for myself, to lift that burning brand placed on *my being*.

Chapter Four

SHIRLEY ANN
SMITH-GORTON-WHITE

My mother, Shirley Ann Smith, was born March 4, 1941, in Boise, Idaho, where most of my grandmother's (Doris) relatives lived.

My grandmother, Doris Smith, was only thirteen when my mother arrived to this young mother. Grandmother (Doris) was too young and unprepared to love a child, which she held in her arms.

Due to the young age of Grandmother, several relatives offered to take care of my mother.

My grandmother (Doris) was plagued by demons who lurked in the dark crooks of my family tree, descending from generation to generation.

My mother endured relentless, horrible abuse whenever my grandmother felt she wanted attention from a male relationship.

Both my mother and grandmother had mental-health issues. I truly believe that there was a severe emotional disconnection to their children that they both bore. Their associations between their thought process seemed loose or disordered. At times, there appeared that Autism (withdrawal into one's self and inner experiences). My grandmother was ambivalent in making difficult decisions. Both grandmother and my mother would allow their emotional defects compass their reasoning with right from wrong, no matter if the selfish act caused pain and grief to others, just as long as they got what they wanted. This thought process affected relationships and damaged their children and grandchildren throughout their lives.

My mother would have severe mood swings. During these mood swings, she could go from happy to sad in seconds. *Love* or *hate* within seconds. No one could predict what or why my mother would say or do. It was extremely hard to be around her. I would always walk softly and quietly too. Usually, this did no good. Mother still would go into one of her rampages. I was never able to judge when or how her blowup episodes would happen.

It seemed that both my mother and grandmother (Doris) might have multiple personality disorders. My mother could go from mild irritation to severe angry mental rage. This could place both my mother and grandmother (Doris) into a category of mental disassociation, lack of social skills.

There would be times when either my mother or grandmother would blow into one of these rages and accuse some one of trying to speak or illustrate dislike to them. This would scare me. I did not know how to exhaust this high level of outbursts.

I hid from my mother. However, she managed to find me. The beatings would begin over and over again.

At the top of my mother's lungs, she screamed and swore, always yelling at me that it was my fault. I did something to cause her outbursts! I began to feel I deserved the beatings and also the cruel words that expressed her hate for me.

The *second central theme* that seemed to organize itself around both my mother and grandmother (Doris) was their world that they both lived in.

Mother used victimization. This allowed her to compass a broad spectrum to reach others to do things for her. More extreme patterns of her destruction, with encouragement of exploitation of abuse to others; loneliness, emptiness, which consisted of a pervasive sense of isolation and distance from the warmth of being part of the human communication, as well as a sense of not having no inner stable self; behavioral pattern underlying the theme of victimization is best characterized.

Being incompetent and contagiousness to others of their sense of emotional intensities.

Looking through my mother's personal papers and diaries, I am stunned at her own reflection of her life, her goals and accomplishments.

Looking into the depths of this woman's soul, thoughts, and reasoning of her actions during her childhood, childrearing, motherhood, and marriages, I witnessed the levels of my mother's maturity, or lack of; my mother's theories of common sense.

Am I judging my mother? *Hell yes!*

Due to her actions and reactions upon her relationships with her husbands, her children, and interactions with family members, I viewed my mother with anger, contempt, and disgust.

My mother wrote her accomplishments as it is listed below.

I noticed my mother's accomplishments were not having children or marriages.

During my research through family members' testimonies, my mother's words written with black ink and her handwriting.

I had to face the facts. There could never be enough sorry, regrets, and excuses to erase the pain. I have made peace within my soul, and I have self-worth. I know I made the correct decision to maintain a distance from my mother and father by miles and years.

I protected my sons, my husband, and mostly myself from my mother's cruel intentions to influence my family unit with negativity.

This was the only way I knew how to keep my mother from harming my family. Stay away from my mother and her poison venom. I wanted the cycle of *child abuse* to end with *me!*

I would not be able to accomplish this feat with my mother's negativity surrounding every aspect of my life.

In my mother's own words, these were her thoughts. I give her all the credit she deserves.

What I Have Accomplished!

1st *Runner-Up*: Mrs. Liberty USA, beauty pageant, 1970s and 1980s.

Mrs. Walnut Valley Beauty Pageant, Walnut, California 1970s and 1980s.

Involved with beauty pageants with Mr. Spillman in the 1980s and 1990s Model Award

Makeup artist, given by Mr. Spillman

Silver Poets Award: Anthology Book 1980s and 1990s. Poem of my dead son's death who died 1974.

(My mother took my poem and revised it as her own)

Wrote and published short stories in the Reader's Digest and other magazines when I was *young.*

Creative-Writing Awards:
have taught English/Writing/ creative writing.

Certifications That I Have Gotten
Mental Health Certification
Certification Nursing Assistant 1976–1988
Sub-teachers certification
Award working on my *Psych Tech/* certification
PTA. Most accomplished award
Award in oil painting in Whitter, California
Perfect Attendance Award, November, December, January, February, and March.
Barrel Racing Award—winning a silver belt buckle.
Training Award for "Horse Training"
Basketball Award given by Mrs. Dawes in Beaver, Oregon, 1950s
Baseball Award given by Mrs. Dawes in Beaver, Oregon, 1950s
Track Awards—short sprint, one-mile run, high hurdles, and low hurdies, 1953
Award in Bible given by Elder McKeowen in Tillamook, Oregon. Certifications and awards given from different Bible studies in the 1950–60s, 70s, and 80s.
Taught painting and ceramic classes *along with watercolors.*
Taught crocheting from time to time since I was five years old

Mother-Shirley Ann Smith-Gorton-White (Kit),
age forty-two, West Covina, California

Chapter Five

FOURTH OF JULY

Fourth of July Parade 1969
Cody, Wyoming
Crystal Dawn Gorton
Age: five years
Unknown names of the two boys
Shirley Ann Gorton on the snow machine

Fourth of July 1969. I was four years old.

I was entered on a Fourth of July parade float.

Dressed in a costume as a mermaid. Wearing a blue tank top, and a foil tin bodice to the toes, a foiled tail molded on a piece of cardboard.

I was placed on a stale, molded, and prickly stray. The four stakes on each side of hay stacks were the illusion of a fish aquarium.

The float was towed by the owner of a towing business that serviced the Park County area.

The sticks of straw dug into my skin, and I squirmed from irritation from being pricked. My eyes watered, and a rash appeared on my arms.

Mother spoke with a warning under her breath, "Smile and wave."

Mother loved being the center of attention, any attention.

I badly needed to use the bathroom. I was scared to tell her. It was too late; my bladder let lose. Pee trickled down my legs and filled up mermaid fin.

"Move your fin and wave. I am not going to tell you again!" Mother said, waving like she was the most important person in the parade.

Mother noticed my bathroom accident. Her nose wrinkled with disgust.

She remained silent until the float turned the corner off Main Street.

"Could not wait 'til you got home?"

Mother was not aware her friend, Marion, had overheard the mother's question.

"Shirley, it is not going to hurt anything and, for sure, not hurt anyone."

Marion had no idea that she caused more of problem by voicing her opinion.

"Don't worry, honey. It is easy to clean up. I promise," Marion tried to reassure me. I knew different. I was so *right*!

Mother gave me a look of, "You are going to regret, and you are in store of a *hell* of a whipping."

Mother walked away, leaving me on the float on the same haystack, which smelled of pee and mold.

After the last float turned the corner off Main Street, I got assisted out of the float.

Mother grabbed my arm with jerk.

Making sure no one would witness her slapping both sides of my face, in a low growl, she said, "You enjoy sitting in your own *piss*?" She pushed me toward the car. She placed a small box on the back seat. "Your name is Little Piggy." She picked me by both arms and placed me inside the box. Closing the lid, my whole body cramped in the box. "You smell like a piggy. So you will learn to like the smell too."

I sat in the box. As she turned corners, the box leaned back and forth. I was afraid I would fall sideways and soil her car.

Unaware that Marion was sitting in the front passenger seat, she said, "*Stop it!* She's just a child!"

Marion tried defending me. Instead, she made it worse. I could tell my mother was getting increasingly madder. The turns around the corners were rougher.

I knew my punishment had not arrived. I was again *right*!

Still wearing the peed costume, Mother told me to put my nose into the doorframe after we got home.

"Don't you dare move, my little piggy!" Mother changed her clothes and put on her house coat. "You stay *right there*! Don't flinch a muscle!"

I tried not falling asleep, but I did fall asleep. My eyes lids grew heavy, my body swayed back and forth.

When my brothers were called to dinner, they both touched my shoulder to wake me up, not saying a word to me; otherwise, they would be in the same situation as me.

Harvey Leroy Gorton Sr.
Crystal Dawn Gorton, August 22, 1964

August 21, 1964

We went into the hospital at 8:30 AM, had a shot at 9:00 AM, and another one at 1:30 PM, and again at 2:20 PM. They broke my water. My labor pains started at 3:00 PM. I had Cris at 10:38 PM this evening.

August 22, 1964

Harvey and Bruce were up to see me for a few minutes this evening. Harvey bought Cris a pink dress.

Harvey, who was my first father on the birth certificate, walked past me. He did not say a word to me, nor asked mother why I was standing in the corner in a mermaid costume smelling like pee. He thought by not mentioning or inquiring about my mother's discipline, he would not make more problems.

"Is Crystal going to remain in the door, or can she have dinner?" he muttered his question.

"Nope, she will stay there 'til I tell her she can move," Mother answered. "She wants to act and smell like a Little Piggy. I intend to treat her as one."

Dinner was over. JR washed the dishes. Mark fed and watered the dogs.

"JR, get the yard water hose and put it through the bathroom window," Mother instructed.

"Okay, get into the bathtub. Time to clean the little piggy," Mother said with a giggle.

"JR, I will tell you to turn the water on, and I will tell you when to turn it off." Mother put the end of the hose into the bathtub.

"Turn it on," she ordered.

The water was chilling cold. When the water was at the halfway mark inside the tub, she again ordered JR to turn off the water.

"Clean yourself up. I am sick and tired of you smelling up the whole house."

Mother stood up from the toilet seat. She went into her bedroom and closed the bedroom door.

Hour after hour I sat in the freezing water, my costume sticking to my wet body.

Finally, Mother came out of her bedroom while the TV blared out the noise of the brutal whipping from her belt through my wet clothing.

"Now clean yourself up. Don't you dare wake up your father. He has to get to work early in the morning! JR, get them into bed. I do not want to any noise from any of you three."

Mother walked to her bedroom.

JR helped me dress in my PJs. He tried not to brush over the welts that started to form over my legs, back, and butt. JR put me in my normal place in the bed I shared with both brothers, right in the middle of the queen-size bed.

JR read me a story from his Sunday-school book. I fell asleep as his voice faded into my dreams.

"JR, they're biting me. Get them away from me!" I was screaming. My dream was now my reality. I could see the stuffed dogs snarling and grabbing my nightgown.

"What the *hell* is going *on*?" Harvey yelled through their closed bedroom door.

"She thinks the stuff dogs are attacking her. She is scared of something bad," JR answered as he tried calming me.

"They are after you, JR! They are *biting me*!" I could see their teeth.

Their fangs were white, and their noses were narrow. The stuffed dogs continued biting me.

"Shirley, get in there and quiet her down. Giver her an aspirin," Harvey spoke harshly, and this angered Mother even more.

"I will take care of this *now*! You bet I will remember this in morning. I will deal with you later! Now get your *ass* to sleep!" Mother said, pointing to me.

After Mother left our room, and we heard her shut their bedroom door, JR brushed my hair from my teared face. He took the two stuffed dogs and threw them inside the closet.

JR. then placed a kitchen chair in front of the closet door.

I stayed awake, fearing the darkness would let the stuffed dogs loose from the closet. Finally, the darkness creeped away, the sun appeared.

JR woke Mark and me, dressing us both. He placed his finger to his lips. JR motioned us outside. We stayed outside for the whole day while Mother slept.

Harvey went to work. Jr, Mark, and I prayed that Mother would forget last night.

Nope! My mother dealt with each of us. We received a beating. The black-and-blue bruises seemed never to disappear because there was always another beating waiting for *us*.

Chapter Six

VISITOR FROM HELL

Grandma Brummett and Step-Grandfather Brummett, my mother's parents, lived in Vancouver, Washington.

Their house stood among the overgrown trees, which hung low onto the winding dusty driveway. The driveway narrowed into a one-car lane. As the road climbed higher through the dense forest, ferns and moss carpeted each side of the steep embankment of the driveway.

A Victorian-style cottage greeted us as we came into the yard. Faded pink paint outlined the broken, cracked screened windows and swinging porch doors. The house slowly rotted due to the damp and continuing misty weather. Even the white chipped paint, which once looked pretentious, was now a victim of the elements of harsh weather.

Mother pulled her white Buick, trimmed with sporty red stripes that matched the red interior upholstery, dashboard, and the inside-door panels, arrived at the end of the driveway.

Mother parked the car, facing the double doors of the barn. The roof beams buckled inward, as the same faded white chipped paint seemed to be the only glue keeping the barn from toppling completely over.

Dry hay laid in the broken stalls. One gray hen still remained pecking at the dirt of this dreary landscape.

Branches clawed at us, like witch's fingers, as we exited out of Buick.

"We are here! Don't you dare tell Uncle Bunky or your Aunts that I am *pregnant*! Not a *damn* word!"

Mother had not started showing, although she was three months pregnant. Morning sickness was the clue that would give her secret away.

"*Yes*," the three of us said in unison.

"There are my babies!" crooned Aunt Carol as she gathered us into a huge hug followed with a lot of kisses.

"How was the drive, Shirley?" Aunt Carol asked my mother while she held my hand and lifted me up and over the broken stone steps.

"Fine. It started raining the second we crossed over the state line into Washington."

Aunt Carol opened the porch screen door. Whicker lawn furniture was situated around the entryway, positioned as if the wicker furniture were armored soldiers protecting the house and fortress against *evil*.

"Bunky and Cindy are in the kitchen drinking ice tea," said Aunt Carol, ushering JR, Mark, and me into the kitchen. She motioned for us to sit at the kitchen table.

She opened the wooden cabinet and retrieved three tumblers, which she then filled with ice tea.

"Drink your tea. There are also oatmeal cookies in front of you." She pushed the plate of cookies in front of us. "Still warm," Aunt Carol said with a smile.

"Do not look at me. Go ahead, get a cookie," Mother said, glaring at us. She still stood at the entrance of the kitchen entryway.

My stomach was growling from hunger. Mother only stopped for gas on our way to Grandparents' home.

"Leave the kids in the kitchen," Aunt Carol instructed my mother as she walked into the foyer.

"Were you able to locate a Ouija board?" Mother asked while she opened the drawing-room doors.

"*Yes*, I did, and I also got six large candles. I could only find red candles though," Aunt Carol replied.

The drawing room's large bay windows loomed over the mahogany ceilings. The wooden floors also showed workman's craft skills of beautiful mahogany, which made the room look larger than what it truly was. Six oversized red velvet chairs circled around the card table. Each red chair was placed uniformed directly in front of a lit red candle.

"Bunky! Cindy! Come on! It's time!" Mother's voice rang out with excitement.

"Who are the extra two chairs for?" Aunt Cindy questioned Mother.

"For our friends!" Mother answered with a slight snicker.

"You do know we are expecting guests?" Mother said while she closed the sliding wooden drawing-room doors.

Each participant pulled out their chair and waited for Mother's signal to sit down.

Meanwhile, JR, Mark, and myself remained in the kitchen, seated the kitchen table. Not one piece of crumb was left uneaten. The cookie plate was spotless.

JR pushed his chair from the kitchen table. He placed his fingers to his mouth and tiptoed onto the wooden floor inside the foyer.

When JR got to the drawing-room doors, he put his ear to the door.

Mark and I stood in the kitchen doorway, watching JR as he used one his hands to wave us back to the kitchen table.

Mark and I paid no attention to JR's instructions to stay away. Instead, we crept quickly down the same foyer that JR was standing on.

Keeping our heads low, we saw JR watching the scene through a small gap in the sliding drawing room doors.

I focused on the lit wick that was dancing in the red candles. The flames kept my attention until my mother's voice broke my trance.

"I command you to enter our circle!" My mother's voice loud as a chill swept along the sides and through the drawing room. The red candles danced faster, flickering like a breeze brushed the flames.

My mother was at the head of the table, my Aunt Carol sitting across from Mother. On each side of them were my aunt Cindy and Uncle Bunky, the two empty chairs on the other side of them.

"Is someone here?" Mother commanded firmly, requesting an answer.

I could see a tall shadow looming over Mother. Then the shadow drifted to the empty chair closest to Aunt Cindy.

I wanted to close my eyes, praying it was only my imagination.

I did manage to open one eye and continued gazing into the candles. But slowly my gaze fell upon the empty chair. *It was not empty!*

An ugly black form with piercing red eyes, thin skin surrounding its sunken eyes, and a grayish skeleton-bone features sat on the once-vacant chair. Its hands formed like eerie tree limbs, which also greeted us as we drove up the driveway. *Its* fingernails scrapped, as if it had daggers, across the Ouija Board. Its mouth growled, bellowed out from *hell!*

"What is your name?" My mother asked, not giving a hint that she was aware of what was sitting next to her.

"How could she not see *it?*" I questioned myself.

No one seemed to see it but me.

I tried moving my legs. Neither leg would or could not budge. I was frozen with *terror*. I was not able to neither move nor speak.

The wooden pointer on the Ouija Board started moving to a letter and spelled out.

The creature's limb was laying on the Ouija Board's pointer. Meanwhile, all four participant's hands laid on the bottom of the creature's hand!

"What do you want?" whispered Aunt Carol.

"*You!*" replied the shadow creature, still pointing out the letters over and over.

Staring at the Ouija Board, I noticed the cardboard turning from white into brown. Crumbling the sides of board into decayed dust. I watched the letters of the alphabet slowly disappearing too. Only faded black ink outlines remained of the *evil*, which was conjured from the Ouija Board, the unspoken words of the dead. At the far side of the Ouija Board printed in large *black* letters were "*Yes*" and "*No*."

"Are you alone?" asked Uncle Bunky, his voice in a deep, confident tone.

The black ink from the Ouija Board became darker and darker as the wooden pointer went straight to the word in the far corner, "*No!*"

Mark's body pushed the two sliding wooden doors farther, and I fell inside the drawing room, tumbling onto JR and Mark both.

When I gained control of my arms and legs, I pulled myself into a sitting position, leaning against the wooden doors, feeling dizzy and nauseated.

No one inside the circle seemed to notice the intrusion. I looked toward the shadow. My vision was blurred. I smelled decayed, rotten eggs and sulfur. The rotten aroma was thick in the stale, heavy air. I wanted to vomit.

My ears pounded to each beat of the chanting that Mother, Aunt Cindy, Uncle Bunky and Aunt Carol started.

Mark and JR also began chanting too.

Was I the only one not caught in this *trance?*

The Ouija board was the center of everyone's attention. They were staring at the board; the wooden pointer was moving without anyone's assistance. The noise from the pointer was moving faster, and the letter Z-Z was spelled out faster and faster. I felt the electric energy running through my veins.

Picking myself off the floor, I launched at the sliding drawing-room doors, hitting the doors just as they slammed shut.

The impact of my shoulder landing against the hard doors brought tears and a terrible, sharp pain throughout my body.

"CALM DOWN! NOW BREATHE!" I heard Mikheal's voice yelling in my head. Slowly my breathing, my tears, and the pain ceased to control my mind and my thoughts.

I was able to see and think clearly. *Now!* I was in control of every part of myself. This *evil shadow* was trying to pass into my body. I had to save myself and my *family!*

Panic and fear was the threat I had to shield my thoughts and soul from this *demon* from *hell!*

Looking up, I saw the *shadow* standing before me.

No words were spoken between us. Only his blazing, fiery red eyes watched me. It had a monstrously huge skeleton frame and unhuman *shadow!* Its eyes were outlined with black darkness, no pupils, only a looming skeleton frame, which hit the wooden ceiling beams.

My heart beat faster. The smell of sulfur was stronger. Its bony finger poked my skull. I remained silent, not *moving!*

The heat from its fingers scorched onto my *flesh!*

The *shadow-demon* ran its fingers down my spine.

My flesh burning with *fire!*

"You don't *fear me?*" The *shadow-demon's* voice shook the walls.

"Who *am I?*" It was expecting an answer. I gave none!

Grabbing my hand with a severe yank, I again I felt the searing burning pain from its iron grip.

Once again, it repeated the question, "*Who am I?*"

"You are very *bad!*" I whimpered, grinding my teeth from the pain.

The energy was draining from the four participates at the Ouija-board table.

Both of my brothers were laying on the floor; there was no *movements*, no *sound*.

All their energy were being drained into the Ouija board as it glowed into a swirl of *fire, glowing* and *forming* as if it was witches' brew.

My energy flowed out of my body, into a mist floating toward the Ouija Board.

I watched the image. Was it a dream? Trying to pull myself from staring into the transparent smoke, I witnessed everyone's inner soul leaving their bodies. I was vanishing into the bright, glowing mist. I felt myself struggle, feeling *Mikheal*, my guardian *angel*, holding me with all his strength!

Mikheal started shaking my shoulders, saying, "WAKE UP!"

Another forceful shake, my shoulders felt the vibration from his hands.

Looking up, I focused my thoughts on Mikheal.

"This is not a *dream*!" Mikheal was screaming inside my head.

I recognized Mikheal's voice!

Feeling myself again, I fought this *battle* to gain control of my life.

Blinking, I could hear Mikheal's booming and thundering *voice*! He was screaming into my brain, my thoughts uniting with his.

"STOP! Stop looking at the *demon*!" Mikheal's shrill tone broke through the trance that the *shadow-demon* held on me.

My concentration no longer listened to the *shadow-demon*. It had lost the grip on my soul.

"Have I broken the *demon's* hold on me? Was I imagining *this*?" I asked myself.

I stood between two of *God's* creatures, *Shadow-Demon* from *hell* and *Mikheal*, my *angel* from the *heavens*!

Smoke! I smelled *smoke!*

The sound of crackling and hissing came from the drawing-room walls, ceiling, and floor.

Trying to push the drawing-room doors to open, I concentrated on getting out of danger, realizing my efforts were fruitless!

I was barely able to breath!

My lungs filled with smoke.

The drawing room was blanketed stronger of the odor of *sulfur*!

Rushing toward the windows, I tried to pry the locks to open.

They would not loosen!

Nothing is opening!

Running to my mother, she was still chanting, this time in a foreign tongue!

Frantic, I shook my Uncle Bunky, desperately trying in vain to wake him out of his trance.

Nothing!

I ran to the other side of the table and said, "Wake up! Please! Aunt Cindy!"

Nothing happened! Aunt Cindy was in a trance. She was still chanting!

"Aunt Carol! Wake up! Wake up!" I was screaming at the top of my lungs!

Nothing was waking them up from their trance!

Still *nothing*! "What is *happening*?"

Thick black smoke's burning heat stung my eyes.

The popping wood fell off the rafters and peeled away the beautiful mahogany from the ceiling.

My head was *spinning*!

Still *shouting*, my voice drummed out by the hissing sound from fiery embers of burning wood.

I'm screaming, but *no one responded*!

Why was no one *listening?*

The only response was deafening *silence*!

A shivering silence!

Evilness was the expression lingering on my mother's face. With her hands hanging motionless limp at her side, her vacant eyes stared into the red flickering candles.

The *shadow-demon* ignored my *shouting*!

Its eyes caught sight of Mikheal's wings. Without warning, Mikhael's wings bashed into the limbs and head of the *shadow-demon,* striking its skeleton form!

Finally, Mikheal's punishing boxing blows into the head of the *shadow-demon*, it's towering figure form began shrinking into a dark-green mist ball. The aura floated out of the drawing room.

The drawing room turned back to normal.

No *smoke*!

No smell of *sulfur*!

Several minutes had passed. There was no evidence of horrible nightmare lingering in the drawing room, nor the participates of seance.

Everything was normal!

The house in Washington, where the Ouija
board was used. Visitor from hell.

Well-behaved children, Cody, Wyoming, January 1967:
middle, Crystal Dawn Gorton, age two and a half; *left,*
Harvey Leroy Gorton JR; *right,* Mark Anson Gorton

Doris Brummett and Jim Brummett, 1974

My mother's letter to Richard A. White

Although my mother was married to Harvey Leroy Gorton Sr at this time, my mother bore three babies that Richard A. White fathered.

Hi,

Will, I have been home five weeks tomorrow.

Sure was a long, old trip, and it sure felt good to get home.

While I was in Oregon, I went out on a forty-foot deep-sea fishing boat. I didn't fish. I was too sick. It rained that day, and the ocean was awful rough. The boat did a lot of rocking back and forth. We went out about twenty-five miles and were out for seven hours. That was the longest seven hours I ever put in.

Took Mark and Cris to the Portland Zoo. They just about walked my legs off. It took up three hours to go through the zoo. The kids sure did enjoy it. There was a train in the zoo, and the kids wanted to ride it. So I took them on that. All in all, we had a pretty good time. I was awful worn out though.

Stayed with my folks in Washington a few days. It was nice to see them. It rained the whole time I was there. We had a nice time and visit.

Stayed in Boise on the way home. I visited with my aunt and uncle there.

Darling, would you finish breaking my mare out? If you could only work with her a couple times a month, it would help. I have gotten her used to the bridle and saddle. I have also sat on her, but haven't walked her out yet. That is what I want you to do. She is real gentle and not too spooky. It is hard, and if she will buck very hard, and if she should, I can't take the chance of being thrown.

I love you, sweetheart, and hope you will call me soon.

Yours for now and always.

(My mother did not mention the Ouija board and evil creature that surrounded *us*. Either my mother refused to acknowledge the demon that she invited into Grandparents' home, or she really did not recall the entire seance. *All* I know for sure, it was the scariest thing I ever saw or encountered throughout my fifty-three years of life.)

Oregon Sea Side, 1968: Shirley Ann Smith-Gorton; *far left*, Harvey Leroy Gorton JR; *front*, Mark Anson Gorton; *far right*, Crystal Dawn Gorton

Visiting Great-Grandma Ada, 1968: *middle—between Mark and Harvey JR,* Mother's boyfriend, Dick; *far right,* Harvey Leroy Gorton JR; Mark Anson Gorton (between Great-Grandma Ada And Dick); *front,* Crystal Dawn Gorton

Jim "Bunky" Brummett, Carol Brummett, Shirley Ann Smith-Gorton, 1965

Chapter Seven

JR's Funeral

CERTIFICATE OF BIRTH

FAMILY HISTORY

Father's full name __Harvey Le Roy Gorton__

Birthplace __Minn.__ Date __12/25/39__

Mother's maiden name __Shirley Ann Smith__

Birthplace __Idaho__ Date __3/4/41__

Residence at time child was born __Cody, Wyoming__

Sex of Child __M__ Weight at birth __8__ pounds __2__ ounces. Length __21__ inches

LEFT   RIGHT

MOTHERS THUMB PRINTS

LEFT FOOTPRINT   RIGHT FOOTPRINT

This Certificate will always be useful in establishing the date and place of your child's birth and the identity of the parents.

Official registration is at

(38)

58

Harvey Leroy Gorton JR, age seven years old, Cody, Wyoming

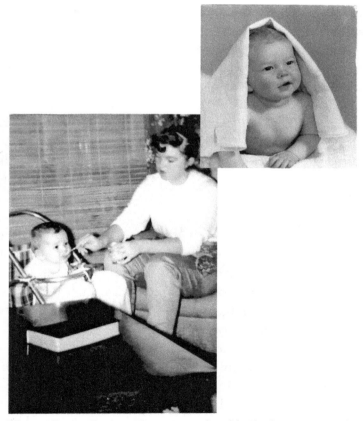

Harvey Leroy Gorton JR, six months old; Shirley Ann Smith-Gorton; Harvey Leroy Gorton JR, September 1958

Harvey Leroy Gorton JR

Harvey Leroy Gorton JR, the *first broken voice*.

Harvey Leroy Gorton JR was born to Shirley Ann Gorton and Harvey Leroy Gorton Sr. on June 14, 1958.

Our mother and Harvey JR's father (Harvey Sr.) married on November 14, 1957, in the county of Tillamook, Oregon. Their marriage ended in a divorce on December 27, 1963.

During their marriage, two sons were born to Shirley and Harvey Mark Anson Gorton, born on May 9, 1962.

During Harvey JR's brief life on earth, I knew about the torment and cruelty. I learned only bits and pieces about his sixteen years. I did know that there were harsh and terrible inflictions Harvey JR endured while in our mother's care.

These are the details I write about the personal account for Harvey JR between ages eight and fifteen; testimonies from relatives who described and also explained the brutal, savage beatings, inhuman, barbaric, and merciless hatred toward Harvey Jr; the adolescent home environment, which Harvey JR learned to adapt to. Harvey JR felt loved and safe with his father and stepmother. Harvey JR's brief teenage years were terminated due to drowning; his death was a tragedy to family and friends on July 30, 1974, a date that also burned onto my heart. Sorrow and grief were the emotions I have for Harvey JR.

Harvey JR's final hour of life ended with his suicide. Although there were several different versions to JR's death on this day of celebration, it was also a day of sadness and mourning, how a young man's life ended way too soon. The outcome still remained the same. A talented, caring, and huge-hearted young man died, Either by his own doing or the will of *God*.

I needed and wanted to give Harvey JR a *voice*, to tell the story about a brother's emotions; his belief that his life was meaningless; how our mother's venom poisoned our thoughts of self-worth. We felt we were *zero*. Mother was pure *evilness*. The family courts instructed Harvey Sr. to share custody with our mother. Harvey JR begged not to be returned into our mother's shared custody. Harvey JR preferred *death*.

Anything, just not to go to our mother's cruel and hatred abuse. *No one!*

No one heard JR's last breath, nor his last words.

Harvey Sr. looked up from watching the ocean waves rolling closer to the picnic cloth laying over the sandy beach. Harvey Sr.'s eyes rested upon Harvey JR just as Harvey JR mouthed the words, "I love you!"

The roaring noise of the ocean grew louder, concealing Harvey JR's struggle from the sand and pebble footpath.

JR tried catching his breath, Tried to run faster into the breaking waves. He was running away from his classmates and relatives. Each wave took him further out into the open arms of the sea.

This would be Harvey JR's last birthday, his last celebration of his life, a farewell gathering among loved ones.

The memories of summer, sandy beaches, and laughter remained like footprint left on the sand, quickly erased by the tides. The sunset hid Harvey JR's looming, ending future.

Harvey JR enjoyed the last hours with his father, stepmother, and classmates on the beautiful crisp afternoon of this day. It started with laughter and birthday wishes, kisses and hugs from relatives. Now it ended with sorrow, falling hearts, and tears.

Harvey JR had no fear as he began his climb over fallen tree limbs, which has anchored itself onto the beach. Harvey JR turned to see his friends and relatives splashing into the waves, rolling onto the sand, witnessing the joyful scene on Oregon ocean beach.

Harvey Sr. said he watched his son smile and wave.

"I love you, Dad!" Harvey Jr said. "Thank you for my birthday party." These were the last words exchanged between father and son. Harvey JR jumped off a boulder that was a hundred yards from the shore. He dived into the ocean.

"I love you too!" Harvey Sr. said, unaware that these were the last words JR would ever hear.

A dying soul, like a Greek tragedy Shakespeare play.

Harvey JR felt the waves comforting him as he watched the reflection of his body disappear into the blue abyss.

The ice-cold sea welcomed JR into the arms of everlasting *peace*.

Harvey Leroy Gorton JR, seventh grade

Harvey Leroy Gorton, freshman in high school

JR's funeral

"*God* shall wipe away every tear from our eyes, and there shall be no more death, sorrow, crying, nor pain. All, can you imagine all the darkness wiped away forever?" said the Pastor to the mourners. "Our Lord loves and cares beyond words. He feels his loved children grief. Our Lod Jesus stretched in arms to us. He wants to cradle our hurt and pain away."

My mother sat straight, her hands gripping the side of the wooden bench. Her eyes stared at the royal-blue coffin. No emotions showed upon her face while the parade of mourners paid their respect, as they wiped away tears; as they passed my parents, giving hugs, and whispering, "Sorry for the loss of Harvey JR" Their final farewell spoken to the closed casket.

"As we gather to remember our beloved son, friend, and Lord Jesus's child, we have wonderful memories of a beautiful soul in our hearts and thoughts. Please remember to give ourselves and turn to *God*."

Mother showed no tears. Emotions of grief were demonstrated with her shoulders heaving into a slumped position against her current husband (Richard White).

Pastor Godwin continued to sooth his congregation with words of hope, love and kindness.

"Harvey JR has left this material world. His presence shall remain in our hearts forever," Pastor's voice echoed through the church walls.

Tears poured from Harvey JR's classmates as they held and comforted each other. One of Harvey JR's friends spoke at the altar.

"I will remember Harvey JR for his quick wit and his caring love to his father. Harvey JR always gave kindness to his friends. He loved his step-sisters, Darcy and Kim. He really enjoyed family meals with his family. He created friendships that stayed strong. He was always willing to help anyone at any time. Harvey JR, I will keep you in my thoughts and prayers."

Keeping his composure, Pastor Godwin's voice trembled and quivered as he bit bottom lip.

"Harvey JR left behind sadness, questions, and turmoil when he joined our Lord Jesus Christ. Together we mourn JR's death." Pastor

Godwin cleared his throat and continued comforting the mourners. "The last days of sadness and mourning—we will comfort each other. We will struggle with believing this young man ended his life, or perhaps an unforeseen accident. Either way, our pain is a brutal loss!" Pastor Godwin motioned for the mourners to rise and join hands.

"We pray for to our Lord Jesus Christ. Take our beloved Harvey JR, our beloved son, Harvey Leroy Gorton JR, into the bosom of our Lord Jesus Christ. Beg *God* to have mercy and peace, forgiveness and understanding."

Mother screeched as the pallbearers carried the royal-blue coffin to the shiny black hearse awaiting to deliver Harvey JR to his resting place.

My mother fell to her knees, pleading for Harvey JR to be returned to her.

"*I love you!*" she said, holding her empty arms around herself. Only emptiness. Her dead son was no longer frightened of her.

"You cannot be dead!"

Every person in the congregation witnessed a mother's grief. But her pleading remained unanswered.

"Give Harvey JR back to me! He belongs to *me!*"

Harvey Leroy Gorton JR, his resting place 'til God places his hands on everyone who will be in the kingdom that Jesus promised to the good and deserving sons and daughters

My Brother

A year ago today, my brother departed.
It is too late now for anything we or say.
We can't erase the sadness, or edit out the tears.
We can't undo the wrongs we've done, we can't relive the years.
The brother that I remember, mistakes that I regret.
You have memories that happened,
I will never forget.
I often wish that life could be the way it was before.
The young days of childhood, the growing pains of youth.
But memories keep building, each one a different kind.
Each one a separate chapter
That is stored within the mind.
My brother is now gone from me.
One remembers now, only a little bit, and pieces.
His laughter mixed with tears.
Now he is lost forever through the years.
This poem, written for a voice that no longer speaks.
His life forever gone from earth, but he is in the angel wings.
Our Lord Jesus Christ, caring arms, loving heart.

A letter written to my mother from grandfather's fourth wife, Christina Smith, regarding JR's death:

August 8, 1974,
    Dear Shirley, Dick, Mark, Cris,
    It is hard to express how we feel at a time like this.

I know what you are going through. I lost a son too. He was six months old. But it is still hard to lose him.

This check is to help with expenses, since we didn't know in time to send flowers, and I am sorry we couldn't go with you.

I think you should tell Cris about her ear, and Mark too, for her protection. I know you didn't want others to know, but we did tell Bill and David. So they wouldn't play to rough with her and look out for her. If you want me to tell her and Mark, I will. I know it is hard to do.

May God be with you and help you through this time of need.

Love, Mom and Dad Smith

Chapter Eight

ATTEMPT TO COMMIT SUICIDE

W. R. Coe Memorial Hospital

Cody Wyoming

This Certifies that _Crystal Dawn Coston_ was born to _Harry and Shirley Coston_ in this Hospital at 10⁵⁵ p.m. on Friday the _21st_ day of _August_ 196_

In Witness Whereof the said Hospital has caused this Certificate to be signed by its duly authorized officer and its Official Seal to be hereunto affixed.

_____
Superintendent

_____
Attending Physician

Crystal Dawn
Gorton, six months
old, Cody, Wyoming

Hanging up
laundry to dry;
Mark standing on
the chair; Crystal
Gorton standing
by Mark, Cody,
Wyoming 1956
1967
Crystal Gorton
holding a puppy,
Cody, Wyoming

Crystal Dawn Gorton, Grade 3 (age seven), first grade, Cody, Wyoming

71

Crystal Dawn Gorton
Age six, second grade,
Riverton, Wyoming, 1970

Crystal Dawn Gorton,
grade third, age seven,
Riverton, Wyoming, 1971

Crystal Dawn Gorton

Crystal Dawn Gorton,
age nine years, Whitter,
California, 1973

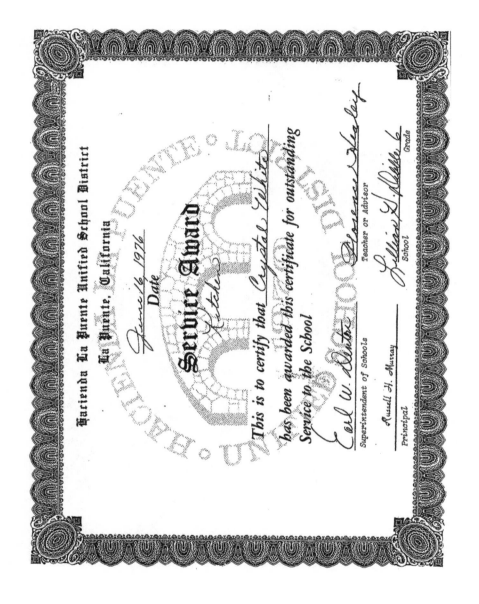

Hacienda La Puente Unified School District

La Puente, California

June 16 1976
Date

Service Award

This is to certify that Crystal White

has been awarded this certificate for outstanding

Service to the School

Earl W. Whitlock
Superintendent of Schools

Russell H. Murray
Principal

Florence Hagley
Teacher or Advisor

Lillian L. Reed
School

6
Grade

Crystal Dawn White,
junior high school,
Hacienda Heights,
California, 1976

Crystal Dawn White,
age thirteen, Hacienda
Heights, California, 1977

At the tender age of eleven, I attend Cederlane Middle Junior High School in Hacienda Heights, California.

On this bright, crisp, fall morning, it was early November. I was sitting on the brick wall next to the Girl's PE locker rooms.

The cool breeze twisted the red-and-gold leaves on a perfect autumn day. The wind created a whirlwind among the branches, only leaving trees with barren sticks, a silent whisper along the abandoned limbs. Harvest of colors warned us winter was upon the next sunrise.

The school bell rang, informing the entire student administration that third period was to begin in six minutes.

Gathering the books I used during second-period class, I rushed to get the books I needed from my locker, which was located near my Social Studies classroom.

In an instant my lower pelvic cramped into a terrible, crushing jab. I doubled over, trying to keep my books blocking the scene that was playing out in front of my third-period classroom. Students stared at me as I tried to inhale deep breaths. I barely walked into the classroom and fell into my desk seat at the far side of the back classroom.

The pain crippled my movements as I sat at my desk.

Staring at the floor, lowering my eyes from other student's gaze, I felt a burning, flush heat in my head all the way to my toes. My Social Studies book slipped to the floor as I leaned down to retrieve the book. I noticed a deep red stain appearing on my baby-light-blue jeans.

A gentle touch tapped my shoulder, making me jump, and again the Social Studies book fell to the floor.

Mrs. Healey, the Girl's P.E. coach stood in front of me. She concealed the embarrassing situation. Putting her arm around my shoulder, she quickly placed the files she was carrying in front of my pelvic area.

"I think you and I should go to the nurses' office."

No reply was needed from me. We walked across the school campus toward the administration building, where the nurse's office was located.

"The other students are too busy getting to their next class to notice you, and my papers are blocking any question that you may get asked," Mrs. Healey spoke softly, keeping our pace at a fast, brisk stride.

We had managed to get the nurse's office just as the second school bell rang, directing the students to be in their classroom and be seated.

"I believe Nurse Kelley will be able to assist you in this very sensitive issue."

Mrs. Healey opened the closed glass door leading to the private domain into a sanctuary guarded from prying eyes.

"Mrs. Kelley, this is Crystal. I believe you can give her tender, loving care and advice. I know you will assist Crystal through a sensitive situation." Mrs. Healey guided me to a chair located in front of Nurse Kelley's desk.

"Of course. Just let me finish up with this last sentence on this medical form. Then I can give Crystal my full attention."

With a slight note marked on the form, Nurse Kelley turned the paper over and looked at me with her full attention.

"Well, I shall leave you in capable hands, Crystal."

Mrs. Healey closed the office door and walked back to her classroom of nervous teenage girls in the PE basketball court.

Nurse Kelley stood up from her desk and gently instructed me to sit on a wooden bench behind a privacy screen, blocking the view from other eyes.

"Well, I think you and I should have a talk. Together we can figure out how I might be able to help you." Nurse Kelley sat down next to me on the wooden bench.

"Let me get you clean towels to wrap yourself while I take your soiled clothes and try to remove the blood stains before the blood sets in. Then I can give you a pair of new underwear and a pad to keep you clean."

She took two white clean towels out the cabinet stashed near the sink.

"Give me your pants and underwear. I will soak them in the sink for a few minutes." Speaking softly and handing me the towels, she then walked back to her desk. Mrs. Kelley kept herself busy, giving me privacy.

"I hope the stains will come out of your pants. I love baby blue. These sailor buttons and style. The row of buttons lining so uniformed."

With a girlish giggle, Nurse Kelley explained she dreamt of being a fashion designer. Due to a huge tuition for fashion design, Mrs. Kelley changed her career choice to medical training. (I am so glad Mrs. Kelley did choose to be a nurse.)

"This underwear has seen better days. I am going to trash them." She was talking more to herself than me.

I was deeply embarrassed to hand Nurse Kelley my torn, holy underwear. The elastic was held by a small piece of cloth. I rolled the underwear into a ball before handing her the garment.

Nurse Kelley, sensing my concerns and embarrassment, shrugged her shoulders.

"Crystal, would you mind if I give you a new package underwear? The days of the week are stitched on the pastel colors. I really do not want to break up the week. Please accept them. You will be doing a huge favor."

Nurse Kelley handed me a pale pink lacy embroidered "Wednesday."

"Yes, thank you. I promise I will take good care of them," I stuttered with tears streaming down my cheeks. My eyes beamed with appreciation for her kindness.

"Now, we need to discuss the physical changes your body is doing. Wonderful and beautiful changes in a young woman's life. I would like to prepare you and explain how, why, and could make your emotions go haywire. The mood swings are part of your body balancing the menstrual cycle." Nurse Kelley inhaled a deep breath then continued speaking softly, "Every woman has a different time for maturity. As well as the structure, physical, and emotions. Yet, as women, we do have the same model. Again, you and I will have different health issues. I would like to give you pamphlet. This should explain more in depth about the things you may have questions about."

Nurse Kelley opened her top desk drawer, retrieving a handful of papers. She stacked them neatly in a yellow folder, placing the folder on the edge of her desk.

"Crystal, will it be okay if I explain the correct way to place and depose of a sanitary pad. I know you are smart. You can read the information. But for now you need to put pad inside the clean underwear."

Nurse Kelley handed me a wrapped sanitary pad while she instructed how to place the sticky strip on the inside of the underwear. Nurse Kelley pulled the screen curtain between us and gave me privacy.

On the other side of the screen, Nurse Kelley explained the do's and don'ts.

"When you change the used pad, which should be every three hours or less—really depends on the blood flow—*never* put the used pad in a toilet. Use the wrapper from pad you are about to replace the old one inside the wrapper and discard it in the trash. Remember, some days will be heavier than others."

"Keep yourself clean and fresh," Nurse Kelley added as a second thought.

Nurse Kelley took a medium brown paper bag out of her cabinet. She filled the brown bag with sanitary napkins.

"This will help get through the first seven days of your period."

At the edge of Nurse Kelley's desk, she had started to pile a first aid kit with articles I needed for my first introduction to the female curse, period. *I am a woman now*, I thought, looking down at my swollen stomach.

"I need to speak with Mrs. Healey. I just realized you have no pant to wear. Hopefully, Mrs. Healey still has the clothes from lost and found from last year PE bin." Nurse Kelley started to open her office door. "I will be right back," she said before leaving.

I could hear her shoes hitting the pavement with a brisk walk. Nurse Kelley headed toward the girl's locker room across the school campus.

Before Nurse Kelley left, she had wrung out my stained, bloody pants. She emptied the blood-red water from the basin and refilled the sink with clean fresh water, placing the stained pants into the basin.

I went to the sink, trying to scrub my pants along the legs and crotch area. Wringing out the pants, I imagined I heard my mother's voice, screaming at me for ruining her pants. I needed school clothes. I would, without her knowledge, borrow her clothes. I made sure to clean and iron the item I wore back into her closet. These pants were ruined, with no way of hiding the evidence.

"You could not help it?" my mother shouted. "You wore my brand-*new* pants! You ruined them. I cannot replace the pants! I cannot afford it! *Do not* think I will buy you new clothes. Why! You cannot take care of your own clothes!"

I still heard her voice in my head. I've been through this subject before with my mother.

This time it is her clothes I ruined.

Remembering my mother's angry voice, the insults regarding my appearance, I have disgraced her. She was embarrassed to admit I was her daughter.

"*Never* taking care of anything. *Always* too selfish to think or care about others! What *a little piggy you are!*" I heard these words over and over from her mouth. Didn't matter *what*, *where*, or why! I was always to blame. *Always!*

I shivered at the thought of my mother knowing what had happened today—*oh god*, starting my *period*!

She would be unforgiving that I began the path to womanhood. She would feel I was trying to take her status as the only beautiful woman in the household. My thoughts were interrupted by Nurse Kelley. She handed me a dark-royal-blue sweatpants.

"I think these sweatpants will fit just right. In case you leak from your period. The dark fabric will hide the blood." I put the pants on. They fit perfectly.

"You can keep them. Mrs. Healey said no one has claimed them from last semester."

Nurse Kelley sat down at her desk. Reading from a slip of paper, she began dialing the phone number.

"I am calling your mother at her job. Explain about the wonderful news." Nurse Kelley held the receiver of the phone, waiting patiently for someone to answer phone. Nurse Kelley wrote in my personal file, documenting the activities on Wednesday, November 1976.

"Hello, may I speak with Shirley White. Yes, it is important. I am the nurse at Crystal White's school. No, Crystal is fine. I need to speak personally with Mrs. White. Thank You. I can hold."

Nurse Kelley's face turned ash gray.

"Mrs. White, your daughter hasn't done nothing wrong. I would, however, like to speak with you in detail regarding a sensitive matter." Nurse Kelley tapped her fingers nervously on the desk.

"First, I need your permission to release Crystal home early. Would it be possible for you leave work to pick her up from school?"

Nurse Kelley lowered her voice, and her gaze focused on the little paper with Mother's work number. I did not hear my mother's reply.

Whatever my mother's response was, it made Nurse Kelley's tone rise, and she reacted with, "Mrs. White, please understand. Crystal started her period.

"It can be traumatic and sometimes unnerving in a young girl's life!"

She was frustrated and annoyed with my mother's demands and the relentless questions of Nurse Kelley's medical résumé. The room was tense.

"Mrs. White, are you coming to get your daughter? If not, I will find other arrangements for her." Nurse Kelley's eyes were tearing, her face flushed red.

"Yes, I can sign Crystal out of school with your permission. How does Crystal get home every day from school? I will make sure Crystal has all the information she needs on this subject." Nurse Kelley smiled at me and gestured that everything would be fine.

"Thank you, Mrs. White. I will send Crystal home immediately. I am sure you need to return to your *busy* day. Goodbye!"

Before the conversation ended, Mother said loudly and very clearly, "Crystal is only trying to get sympathy and attention. I would not be surprised that she stuck something in her vagina, if you know what I mean?" chuckling as she hung up her receiver. My mother had made an enemy from Nurse Kelley's face, written with, "Your mother is *nuts!*"

Nurse Kelley's hands were trembling, either with anger or disbelief.

"Crystal, you did nothing wrong. *Always, always* remember this!"

"Hello, Joyce. We are sending Crystal home. No, she will have to walk home. Yes, this is how Crystal usually goes home!"

Nurse Kelley explained the conversation between my mother and herself to the attendance secretary.

"Joyce, I could not believe a mother is so cruel. If you heard the things Mrs. White implied, you would be *pissed* too."

Turning her attention back to me, she said, "Crystal, I will write a note to your mother. Then I will escort you off school campus. Please call me if you need anything. *Anything!*"

Nurse Kelley walked me through the administration office.

"Nurse Kelley, may I speak with you privately? Please?"

Mrs. Joyce Steinburg was the administration secretary over twenty years. Mrs. Steinburg became aware of my home environment with gossip from students and their parents. She gave me a sweet smile before talking in a whisper between herself and Nurse Kelley. They were out of hearing range. I watched both of their expressions.

"Crystal White will be excused from school for the remaining classroom periods."

Nurse Kelley nodded in agreement.

"What did Mrs. White say? You are ready to tear Crystal's mother into little pieces." Mrs. Steinburg tenderly caressed Nurse Kelley's arm to show that Mrs. Steinburg understood the frustration that Nurse Kelley was feeling.

"Mrs. White does not feel this is important to leave her job, even for a couple of hours. Yes, she could leave work, if it was truly important. She is pure *evilness!* Mrs. White concluded our discussion, stating that Crystal wanted attention. Therefore, she took a stick, something, and pushed it into her vagina. This is why she started bleeding!" Nurse Kelley gulped then inhaled a deep breath. Catching her next breath, Nurse Kelley continued with the events of the conversation.

"What the *hell* is wrong with that woman?" Not expecting an answer, Nurse Kelley, walked to me.

"Take this note to your PE teacher tomorrow. This will excuse your participation in the activities for the rest of the week." Nurse Kelley handed me a slip of yellow paper folded neatly.

Opening the administration-office door, Nurse Kelley stopped, turning toward me, and said, "Crystal, your body is changing. You have nothing to be ashamed of. When I started my period, my mother explained everything to me and then slapped my face. A Jewish tradition between daughters and mothers. 'This is to remind you that you are a woman today,' and I never forgot that day. It is a step to achieve another stage toward adulthood." Nurse Kelley hugged me.

"If you have any questions, please come to my office. My door is always open."

I stepped into the November air, feeling the sun's warmth upon my flesh, a new stage into womanhood.

It was 10:30 AM. Between the cramping, and hungry pains, I was relieved to have the rest of the day to myself.

I felt the urge of needing to pee. I walked even at a faster pace.

My brisk walk only seemed to make me need to pee worse.

My thoughts went back to being hungry. Missing lunch, *damn*, I liked the corn dogs and french fries that were being served today at lunch.

A warm sensation of liquid ran down my leg into my shoes. The noise of squeaking, squishing sound squeaked with every step.

"Only a few blocks 'til I get home," I whispered to myself.

My heart stopped as I turned up into my driveway. My feet froze in place, and tears filled my eyes.

Mother was *home*! I touched the hood of the car, still *hot*. Mother must have just arrived.

"*Mother, Mother?*" I called as I opened the front door.

Searching each room, moving cautiously, I finally reached my bedroom door. There was Mother, sitting on the edge of my bed. She was lightly smoothing the material of the bedspread with her hands. Next to her was a box of tampons.

I totally forgot that I had peed my pants. I was terrified that Mother was home.

"I told my boss I needed to get home. My daughter was sent home from school with health issues." Mother rose to her feet and handed me the box of tampons. "My boss gave me these to give to you. One of the freight trucks was overstocked. My boss asked me to tell you that he hopes you feel better."

As Mother handed me the box, she stiffened and sniffed the foul smell of urine accident.

"You smell like *pee*! You peed yourself!" She snickered, and her gaze fell upon the brown paper bag I was holding. She took the brown bag from my death-grip hold on the bag. Dumping the contents on my bed, she rummaged through the items: a package of pastel-colored underwear, sanitary napkins, and detailed information about menstrual development.

Expecting the underwear, she said, "You got new under panties? And look at this. You already messed up the pair you are wearing." She pointed to the pants I was wearing. "I do not remember buying you those!"

"You are going to wear those same underwear and smelly pants that smelly with *pee*! *Oh*, and those pads, just forget about ever using them. You are to use the tampons that my boss gave you. *Do you understand?*"

She yanked my hair, pulling my face into my knees, breathing the smell of pee.

"Guess I will have to explain to your husband the reason why his bride is not a virgin is because you love sticking things into your *pussy?*"

She chuckled, the evil sound freezing my soul. She turned my face toward hers.

I tried to keep my eyes staring at the carpet.

"Mike Sr., a friend of mine who lives in Canada, is coming over. And his son, Mike JR" She walked to the bedroom door.

Mike Sr. and my mother started their affair a few years ago. Mother always enjoyed new relationships with variety of several men. Her need for attention from different styles of companionship. But soon, she would weary and tire of boredom with their meddlesome questions. Then another relationship began with another married man.

No strings!

No ties!

I noticed my father's absences became longer, and fewer visits at home.

Father drove an 18-wheeler, long-haul over the forty-eight lower states (truck driver). He enjoyed his hermit and solace inside his truck. He preferred staying and sleeping in the cab of the truck (sleeper) than being at home.

My life at home was always worse with his absence.

My mother shouted and yelled at me, "You are the reason your father *hates* to come *home*! Because you are *brat*. He never wanted a *brat* to begin with! He begged me to abort you! I tried too! Look at *you*! A disgusting, smelly, and piggy *brat*! Your father despises and *hates* to even look at *you*! You are as worthless as a piece of *shit*!"

I quietly slipped into the adjoining bathroom. I pulled off my soiled, peed clothes.

After filling the bathtub with warm water, I washed my body. I placed the dirty underwear and sweatpants into the tub. When I finished scrubbing myself, I scrubbed the clothes using the bar of soap. Pulling a towel around my waist, I quickly walked through quiet house.

As the hall clock echoed, I paced my steps with the beat of the chimes. I placed my wet clothes over the backyard fence. I scurried back to the safety of my bedroom, removing one of the weekday embroidered underwear, Thursday. I put on soiled yet not-smelly pants on. I prayed my mother would not notice the change of clothes.

"Crissy, when Mike gets here, *wake me up*! If he brings his son, JR, keep JR busy," Mother's voice demanded. No questions allowed.

Mother had just begun her ritual of terror, starting with her favorite Highball Whiskey Sour Liqueur drink.

Now on her second glass of Highball Whiskey. Sour.

"I am going to lay down. So keep quiet. You better stay by my side in case I want another drink."

Mother's fingers twirled the ice cubes in her glass, as if telling the future of tornado about to touch down. I perched myself on the top stair leading down to the round bed where my mother slept. A silk Japanese screen separated the pallor landing from the sleeping area.

I felt nauseated, and the cramping started again. These cramps made me double over.

"When was the last time I ate?" I questioned myself.

The last meal I had eaten was yesterday during school lunch.

My mother's snoring—what a peaceful sound. It alerted me when mother woke up. I will rest a bit.

Bang!

Bang!

The thundering sound coming from the front door.

Rushing to the front door, I expected to see Mike standing on the other side of the front door.

Oh shit!

My father stood with his hands full with his carrying case and logbooks. He was as surprised at seeing me as I was at seeing *him*!

"Why are you *home*? Today is a school day, *right*?" I did not answer, and he did not expect one either.

His puzzled look turned into a smile. He saw Mother laying on the bed. He walked toward Mother's slumbering body.

"Hello, honey. I was able to drop the load early and surprise my beautiful wife."

Leaning over Mother, kissing her forehead, Father waved me to leave their bedroom.

I stood at attention by their bed. Not until my mother instructed me to leave, I am to remain right there at her side.

"Rich, you're home!" she said with a fake laugh.

"Honey, why is Crystal home? And you, home? Are you okay? Is Crystal okay?" Father touched my mother's arm gently.

"Well, my dear, Crissy was sent home because she started her period. Being a loving, earing, and concerned mother, I wanted to be here with Crissy." Mother's gaze moved toward me, daring me not to say a *fucking* word, or else!

"*Now*, boys and men will flock all over her like a *bitch* in heat. Wait 'til the dogs sniff after her." Mother grabbed my forearm, digging her finger nails deep into my flesh.

My father stared at her with disgust, his expression turned into anger. As soon as he walked into their bathroom, Mother waited to hear the bathroom door close and the shower water turn on.

"What the *hell* am I to do *now*? Mike will be here any minute."

My mother spoke in a low tone. Her hands still bared her fingernails into my arm. Her clutch tightened into my flesh. She pushed me hard away from her, and I staggered onto the stair.

"You better not move from that spot. *Do you understand?*" Her breath smelled like whiskey.

About this time, my father had exited from the bathroom, naked and unaware I was still in their bedroom.

"Kit, why is she in our room?" My father pointed at me.

He placed the towel over his nakedness.

I kept my eyes focused on the white shag carpet. I turned toward my mother for an order to leave the room.

My father continued, "Why does this room and bathroom look like a tornado came through here? Your clothes are everywhere, makeup lying all over the sink counter. Look at the closet! How in the *hell* can you live like this?"

My father walked to the half-opened closet doors. He was staring at the thrown clothes laying on the bottom of the closet. Some of the clothes half on and off hangers. Mother's shoes and scarfs scattered throughout the pallor room.

My father sprinted to the mother's vanity table, knocking makeup and throwing perfume bottles, hairbrushes onto the floor.

Then with one swoop, he tossed the vanity table over. The seat matching the table crushed beneath the wreckage. Two of the seat's legs broke in half from the impact.

The bedroom was totally *chaos*!

Usually, before Mother arrived from work, I would clean up the disaster mirroring a hurricane: making up the beds, hanging the clothes on wooden hangers, and straightening the scattered makeup, hairpins, everything in its place.

But today both my mother and father came home early.

My father came home unexpectedly. I had nothing cleaned, nothing done.

I still dared not to move. Not until I was instructed to by my mother.

I did not budge or move a muscle!

I still did not *move*!

"Well, honey, maybe she wants you to *fuck* her? After all, she is a *bitch* in. heat. Or maybe it is you who wants to *fuck* her!" My mother's speech slurred, as stubbled approaching my father.

"GET OUT OF HERE!" My father pulled me to my feet.

I remained frozen.

"Well, Rich, this must be what your daughter wants! Her budding, young breasts. The smooth, flat stomach. Shit, I would want her too!"

Mother shoved me into my father's stomach. A burst of laughter roared from her throat. She yanked my father's towel away from him.

I did not flinch!

Showed no signs of *fear*!

My mother loved to make me flinch. Another reason to hit me.

"*Do not* show emotions!" I repeated to myself.

"Oh, I know. Maybe Crissy wants to watch us *make love*! Show her the correct way to have *sex*!" Mother's voice was purring.

My father's eyes narrowed, his anger making him shake.

"Get the *hell* out of *here*!"

I ran out of the bedroom as the last word was shouted.

Their yelling and shouting began behind the shut bedroom door.

My mother's and father's voice became louder and louder.

Within an hour, the voices became silent.

Their bedroom door pulled open. My father left, carrying his overnight bags and trucking logs. His long strides ushered from the house.

His last words spoken to my mother were, "I will be in my truck. Maybe you will come to your senses. You know where find me. When you do, *sober up*! You smell like a stale brewery!"

I listened to my father's footsteps stomping all the way to his 18-wheeler truck parked next to the house. My father's truck sounded angry and growled, as if mimicking my father's exasperation toward my mother.

"Now, maybe I can get dressed and have plenty of time to meet with Mike." Mother's voice squealed like a teenager in high school.

"*Crissy! Crissy*, clean up this mess. I still need your help to get ready." Mother skipped around her bedroom. She twirled around as she decided which outfit to wear.

My head was throbbing with a headache. My stomach cramps getting worse. It felt like a crowbar prying my inners apart. But the worst was the lower back throbbing.

I could not complain.

I will not *complain!*

While my mother took her shower, I took the aspirin bottle from mother's night stand. First, I tapped out one tablet.

Second tablet...

Third tablet...

I did not stop taking the aspirin until I reached fifty tablets, taking five tablets at a time.

I washed down the pills with the whiskey from my mother's glass.

Taking the fifty aspirin tablet, I left the bottle empty.

It did not take long for the aspirins and whiskey to take effect.

My eyes felt heavy, and I swayed from side to side, feeling sleepy. I held onto clothes and hangers inside the closet. Thinking I should reorganize mother's makeup, I turned her vanity table upright. Unfortunately, one of the legs was broken into two. It was not fixable. The vanity mirror cracked and, like a web, crossed across through the middle. There was definitely no way to repair the vanity table.

I was not able to *stop* swaying back and forth, side to side; my eyes blurred. My head felt huge and heavy. My head pounded like a jackhammer, slamming with unbearable vibration through my body.

Resting my head against the broken vanity table, the coolness of the wood soothed my temples. My mother's screeching voice pierced like fingernails scratching a chalkboard.

"Get *up*! You are so useless, not worth a penny." My head felt like cotton balls.

"You are *lazy*!"

I did not feel her fingernails slicing into my forearm. She pulled me with her to the closet. I was not able to walk to her closet. I could not feel my feet moving beneath me. I was weightless.

I could not hear *anything*!

My body crumbled as I hit the floor.

"Go to *your* bedroom. I will take care of you later!" My mother's mouth was moving.

I heard *nothing*!

I know I saw mother's lips moving!

I still heard *nothing*!

"Probably better you stay home. Now, get your *lazy ass to bed*!"

I pulled myself off the bedroom floor, using my hands to guide me into my bedroom.

Slipping between the sheets on my bed, I glazed at the evidence of today's hurricane spread across my bed: brown paper bag with sanitary napkins, box of tampons, and the package of pale-colored underwear scattered on the bedspread.

Pulling the bedspread over my swollen, bruised, and scared body, somehow I felt safe.

"NO ONE CAN HURT ME EVER AGAIN!"

I mumbled to myself as I was engulfed into a dark slumber.

Mikheal, my guardian angel, wrapped his beautiful, soft feather wings around my fragile body. He gently brushed my hair with loving hands. My hair was soaked with sweat and fever.

My tears were visible on my pillowcases.

"I told you, I will always be here for *you!*" Mikheal's voice was a soft melody of music whispered into my ear. I could hear him?

Mikheal's voice was a beautiful melody of soft music.

"Why can you not stop my mother and brothers?" Mikheal knew what I meant. I curled myself further into a fetal position.

"I do not possess the power to *stop* people from hurting each other. Nor can I change the direction of human's choices." Mikheal cradled my head and spoke with a heavy heart.

"I can talk with you and help you. Hopefully, others will make better choices. Only *you,* just you, have the power to change your actions."

I could not comprehend what Mikheal meant.

"*How* can you be a guardian angel if you cannot make the pain go away?" I heard my words spoken into his thoughts.

"You think trying to *stop* the pain is taking your own life? I will not *stop* you. I can, however, be here for you. Sooth your soul. I am not able to stop you from fatally taking digesting the pills. I can *only* talk with you. Perhaps, keep you awake. Keep you from going into a death slumber. I know you feel drowsy. *I need you* to help *me save you!*" Again, Mikheal brushed my hair from my sweaty forehead. "You will and have the power to change lives. You will hear their drowning *voices.* Only you will be their strength. Be strong for *them. Never, never,* forget I am here by your side. I will be your voice. A voice you *hear* in your thoughts. Just before you think or do anything that is *wrong!* I will be your conscience! If you pretend *not* to *hear* me, I will *scream* inside your *mind!* Yet you are still able to make a terrible decision. These are your actions, your decisions, *not mine!*"

I fell asleep with Mikheal's angelic wings surrounding me. I felt *safe,* hearing his caring voice caressing my troubled thoughts, even though my head was a fog filled with cotton balls. The aspirin tablets were making it increasingly impossible to form any thought or speak.

I heard Mikheal!

It was several days before the aspirin ceased making my head feel like cotton balls.

I did enjoy the silence. Not hearing my mother's screams or cruel insults, I actually felt the ground again. My feet touched the floor. I no longer felt like I was floating.

This would be last time I tried to end my life with pills. *Give life a chance!*

Believe *me!* Mikheal continued yelling inside my thoughts!

Mikheal was always close, *never* leaving my side.

I know my heart and soul was protected by *God, Lord Jesus Christ, Holy Spirit, and Mikheal, my dear guardian angel!*

Truck stop Mother worked, Alamanda, California, 1977
Mike, Canada truck driver

Chapter Nine

MOTHER'S VOICE

By the time my Mother turned two years old, my grandmother (Doris) left my grandfather (Merton "Bud" Smith) during the middle of World War II. My mother started calling the gentlemen that grandmother introduced as either Uncle or Daddy.

My grandparents' marriage was filled with chaos. Their relationship was on and off. They were unable to stay married. Every couple of weeks my grandmother threw my grandfather out, or my grandfather tossed my grandmother out. No matter what, it was a roller-coaster ride for my mother, extremely confusing for a child.

Sometimes my mother lived with grandmother (Ada) who was my great-grandmother. My mother felt unloved and told that she was not unwanted.

"Oh, why didn't you die?" Cruel and tormenting words were expressed to my mother from both parents, parents who were to protect and love with joy and happiness, give peace in their daughter's heart. Instead, my mother was treated like a discarded rag doll.

I listened to stories about my mother from her sisters (my aunts) also other family members, speaking in detail regarding my mother's harsh life during her childhood. I began writing my story. I was angry toward my mother. I felt *hate*. My heart was blackened due to my mother's the lack of *love*, which was uncapable to show me. Soon I began to understand my mother's sadness, her darkness, and emptiness in her heart. Most of all, I learned to *forgive* my mother.

I *deserve* to live in *peace*. *I deserve joy*. Most importantly, *I deserve* to be *loved*. My sons showed me unconditional love. I *stopped* the circle or cycle of abuse. Believe me, I am far from being a perfect mother or wife. I am continuing to learn about being a mother, wife, and grandmother.

There will always be difference of opinion, yet through it all, there will always be *love*.

I heard so many stories about my mother's upbringing. I am truly sad, and I do feel empathy for my mother. I felt my mother needed to be heard. Give her a voice!

My mother deserves a *voice*!

Most of my mother's childhood were engulfed with fear and terror. The fear my mother felt was overwhelming pain, and sadness filled my mother's childhood. Days, weeks, and months, and torture. Even male friends of my grandmother were given permission to discipline and molest my mother. Usually, the razor strap was the choice of a beating instrument. Always an excuse for mother's beatings was not finishing her chores.

Another form of punishment was the dark, empty closets. The scary dungeon became a torture chamber to remind my mother her life was filled with goblins and witches. *Evil!*

The corner of the doorframe was also another tool of punishment, a constant reminder that my mother wished she wasn't born.

My aunt told me about the time that my grandmother threw my mother against the wall—my mother was only a few weeks old—because my mother would not stop crying, which angered a young mother of thirteen years old.

"Shut up!" My grandmother yelled louder and louder.

This made my mother cry louder too. My great-grandmother rescued my mother from the brutal inflictions on an already bruised, bleeding infant. She cradled her to sooth the hungry baby.

Sometimes when my great-grandmother was not around, my grandmother would smack, pinch, and kick my mother as hard as she could.

My aunt said she caught my grandmother screaming and flinging my mother into the bed, shouting, "I will *kill* you! Shut up!"

My aunt was shocked and removed mother out of harm's way.

My aunt was really my great aunt on my grandmother's side of the family.

During one of the brief times that my grandparents moved back into a family unit, my grandfather witnessed another episode of his wife's rages against my mother.

He ran to the crumbled heap of dirty clothes in the corner of the bedroom wall. In the pile, my mother was covered over, to conceal the child wrapped in a towel. The towel hung tightly around my mother's neck, and there was no movement. My mother's face was a shade of light-blue/gray color.

My grandfather carried the unresponsive toddler to his car. Rushing through traffic lights, rubbing my mother's chest, coaxing her to talk and open her eyes, he carried her limp body into the hospital emergency entrance.

The medical staff questioned my grandfather about how this young toddler had a bruise around her neck, the welts on her tiny legs, skeleton shoulders, and the butt all the way to her toes, scars upon scars. The outline of a strap still colored with red, blue, black, and yellow bruises.

My grandfather explained that a young high-school teenager was babysitting his daughter. When he arrived home, he searched for his daughter. This was how he found her.

The doctor said, "These injuries are not from one incident. A caring person would not leave welts and scars on a defenseless baby."

My grandfather guaranteed the doctor and medical staff that this would never happen again. Therefore, the medical staff did not report or question him anymore.

My grandfather was very wrong. It did happen. *No one spoke up!*

My mother grew into a beautiful woman.

My mother feared and hated my grandmother.

My mother stepped into my grandmother's footprints.

The circle or cycle did not stop with my grandmother or my mother.

Another story I was told from my great aunt was, my mother was babysitting at seven years old to her sister from another father. My mother was instructed to stay with her sister and change her baby sister's diapers when they were soiled. Also, make sure the baby was fed when she became hungry.

My mother resented her siblings. She knew they were loved and cared about more than my mother felt. There were never any emotions of love given to my mother. She only felt *hate.*

My mother became a mother at seven, being the caretaker to the other siblings born. My mother did not have a childhood, teenage life, and most of all, a stable, loving mother.

My mother endured mental and physical abuse.

I listen to my inner self, and I learned that abuse will cause abuse unless you change the direction.

My mother failed her children, and no, she cannot change this fact. Nor can she change the scars that you cannot see. The scars were so deep in my heart and mind.

I know in my heart and soul, I tried to be a good mother and a good wife. There were times I know I could have done better as a mother and wife.

All I can do is to keep going upward and acknowledge my mistakes. Ask for forgiveness, and stay on the moral compass. Faith is my arrow to the *heaven's gate. I pray I will be in God's graces.*

Shirley Ann Smith, age fourteen years, Boise, Idaho Grandma Ada and Uncle Tom, Boise, Idaho Grandpa…third husband, 1965 Shirley Ann Smith

Shirley Ann Smith
Gorton White, freshman
in high school

Shirley Ann Smith Gorton
White, age thirteen

Chapter Ten

MY GRANDFATHER'S RETURN HOME FROM THE ARMY

My grandmother (Doris) was severely abused by my grandfather (Merton, Bud Smith). Usually, heavy drinking was followed by closed fists, slamming into my grandmother through, or cracking the wooden panels on the walls and floors. Violent kicks were aimed into grandmother's unborn child. The traumatic abuse of each hit or kick caused spasms from inside the womb.

My mother was born March 4, 1941. Her life began with a twist of *evilness*. Her hell was baptized not with Holy Water, but with an assault on her fragile, newborn body. My mother was tossed into the dysfunctional home.

Family members explained to me about my mother's childhood.

I do not want this story to give my mother a pass or excuse for her abusive actions upon her children. However, it did explain her lack of parenting skills.

Behavior is taught by example: seeing, hearing, and repeating the mannerisms that have been witnessed.

My mother's behaviors were not only influenced from her parents, but also the social environment she lived in. Keep secrets.

My grandmother (Doris) moved back in with my grandfather (Bud-Merton Smith).

My grandfather bought a large Army tent. He placed and put it together on the outside of town limits of Boise, Idaho.

My mother and her parents lived inside the tent during the hot summer of July and August. The tent protected them from the sunny and humid days. The floor was bare dirt, dead grass, and gritty straw. Also, crawling bugs found refuge inside the tent. Bugs climbed inside the bedding, leaving sores and red rashes with bumps, which remained untreated on the three occupants.

My mother's chores included keeping the makeshift floor clean from infested bug straw and weeds that grew inside the Army makeshift home.

My mother, only a toddler of age four, figured out how to maintain a clean dirt floor using a simple broom. It was a never-ending job of sweeping throughout the day. There were always miscellaneous debris. My mother's arms felt heavy from continuously sweeping. Blisters turned into callous on her tiny hands.

Since there was no plumbing, just an outhouse as toilet stood a few yards from the makeshift tent. On hot and humid days, the smell from the outhouse became unbearable. The half-moon etched onto the outhouse door was the only source of fresh air inside the toilet.

A wooden seat sat loosely on a spelter wooden box, concealing a round hole dug into the earth. On this evening, no breeze, only the sounds of chirping from the crickets.

My mother was left alone, while my grandparents went into town.

My mother needed to use the outhouse; she was scared to use it when no one was at home. Glazing at the toilet paper my mother held in her small hands, my mother became nervous that she would use too much of the toilet paper.

Although my mother was being very careful not to use too many sheets off the toilet roll, the toilet paper fell into the open hole below the wooden seat.

My mother was in a state of fright. She was instructed to only take a few sheets of toilet paper, not to take the whole roll into the outhouse, just for the reason of losing it.

Any other parent would and could understand that children do and will make mistakes. Of course, a child should have listened. Who was caring for this four-year-old toddler? Not her parents! Leaving a small child alone within harm's way. Unsupervised! The blame belongs to the parents.

My mother tried unsuccessfully to retrieve the roll of toilet paper. Without any success, she feared and shook and trembled harder when my grandparents returned home.

My mother knew that she was going to receive a beating and tongue lashing.

She relived the last beating over and over again in her mind. My grandmother used a large wooden spoon. Scars and welts showed through the thin cotton, linen summer dress my mother had worn for the last weeks—my mother's only dress she owned. Even the sandals Mother wore were too small. Her tiny toes hung over the front of her sandals.

Trying to calm and tell herself, maybe this time her punishment will not be so bad. Maybe Grandmother would not notice.

Thoughts of running away engulfed my mother's mind. Too late. My grandparents drove up to the makeshift home.

My grandfather sectioned the tent into three separate rooms. The mismatched sheets hung over rope to give privacy for Grandparents' bedroom. The kitchen was in full view of mother's cot, which was tucked to the farthest wall at the opening of the tent flap.

My mother hid under the torn blanket on her cot. Cowering from the announcement that my grandfather was already drunk, his booming voice ripped into the still-hot air.

The sun even tried to disappear from my grandfather's slurred words as he demanded supper.

The moonbeam dipped into the dying sun ray and lit my mother's small frail body to the drunk couple. Mother's tears smeared on her red cheek. Keeping her eyes closed, she hoped they would fall asleep soon.

"Shirley, where the hell are you?" my grandfather started speaking louder with each word.

Mother peeked from the corner of the cot and said, "I am here, Daddy."

Walking toward my grandfather, she waited for a command or gesture of affection from her father.

My grandmother headed toward the outhouse. My mother began to shake and cringe with terror. Grandmother searched for the toilet roll.

Now, I am going to get it. My mother's thoughts were praying for a miracle. *No* miracle came, only my grandmother's shrill voice.

"Where is it, Shirley?"

My grandmother yanked my mother's arms forcefully. Using her other hand, my grandmother slapped my mother's face.

My mother's arm stung from the fingernails poking into her delicate flesh.

"Where is it? You know exactly what I am asking for!"

Grandmother shook my mother's body violently. Amazingly, my mother's head stayed on to her shoulders.

"I knew I couldn't trust you by yourself."

With all her strength, my grandmother shoved my mother into the cast iron stove. Her head fell against the open door of the stove, leaving a gash and blood mixed together stuck to the oven door. My mother was stunned from the impact of both the hitting the cast iron stove and the stinging of my grandmother's slap.

"It fell into the toilet," my mother whispered.

Another slap hit my mother's cheek, but this time, Grandfather caught my mother before she landed onto the dirt floor.

My grandfather loosened his tight grip on my mother's arm then settled her back in front of my grandmother's wrath of anger. Grandfather instructed my mother to go to her cot and remain there until the morning.

"Leave Shirley alone!" my grandfather ordered my grandmother.

Grandfather picked up his army hat and brushed off his uniform pants. Walking away from scene of chaos, Grandfather climbed into the driver's seat inside the car. This would be the last time my mother saw or heard from her father 'til 1957.

When my grandfather left, my grandmother's fury was unleashed. My mother was accused of making my grandfather leave. The absence of father and husband became a burden for my mother to carry.

My mother remained silent. She learned to show no tears or emotions, especially when my grandmother whipped, hit, and kicked my mother into a ball, who cowered and covered her head during cruel assaults onto my mother's body.

My mother believed it was all her fault that her father stayed out of her life for so many years. My mother's guilt was not hers to carry.

Merton "Bud" Smith,
age twenty-one
Age twenty-two
Army

Doris Smith (age
fourteen); Merton "Bud"
Smith (twenty-three)
World War II

Shirley Ann Smith, age between two and three, Boise, Idaho

Chapter Eleven

GRANDFATHER'S RULE

When my grandfather divorced his wives, if there were children from the union of this marriage, the children were not to have no any contact with other half-sibling from other marriages. This was grandfather's way of keeping the children silent from comparing the abuse to each other.

For example, when my grandfather divorced his second wife, there were two brothers and two sisters. No corresponding or even a letter was to be allowed to exchange between siblings.

My mother did receive a letter from my grandfather's second wife.

> Shirley,
> Ricki should be home Monday, January 18, about 10:00 PM. I know that her and Chuck, who is your half brother, would love to see or hear from you before you leave Grand Junction, Colorado.
> I sure hope everything works out for you this time. I am only sorry that you and I can't see or talk to each other while you are here, but if this is the way everyone wants it, I guess it is for the best.
> May *God* give you all the happiness in the world.
> Don't forget to call Chuck and Ricki before you leave.
> All my love, even if you're not my girl anymore. Live in peace and happiness.
> *Love, Dee.*
>
> P.S. Please don't say anything to anyone about this, as I am not to get in touch with you anymore.

My grandfather wanted to keep family members away from each other. This was his control and power. He didn't want siblings to compare notes about the molestation that the girls were keeping silent. Keeping his *secret!*

Grandfather also kept ex-wives in line with abusive and controlling system. Keep your mouth shut, or else you would feel the end of his belt and the buckle... Believe me, his wives, past and present, did not reveal the secrets. Even through his death, they never spoke against him or about the hardships he inflicted upon his children.

My grandfather was the *devil.*

His secrets I no longer *keep.*

He had no morals, self-worth, and most of all, he had no *power* or *control* over *me!*

Garden of the Gods, April 5, 1959, Grand Junction, Colorado *top right,* Dolores "Dee" Smith; *far left,* Gloria Smith; *second to left,* Charles Smith; *front right,* Jerry Smith, half brother and sister to Shirley Ann Smith-Gorton

Dee Smith, second wife to Merton "Bud" Smith; Grandfather Merton "Bud" Smith; Step-Grandmother Dolores Smith; *front middle,* Harvey Leroy Gorton JR; *far right,* Mark Anson Gorton; *front left,* Crystal Dawn Gorton

Grandmother Christina "Chris" Smith (fourth wife), 1970
Grandfather Merton "Bud" Smith, second husband
for Christina Smith, Whitter, California, 1970

Chapter Twelve

GRANDFATHER'S DEATH

The last time I saw my grandfather Smith was at the hospital for his liver and heart failure. February 1981.

Request Information
Merton Smith
Residence: 90716 Hawaiian Gardens, Los Angeles, California
Last-
Benefit:
Issued: MI-(Before 1951)
Born 11 December 1919
Died February 1981

Standing over my grandfather's lifeless body in the intensive care unit, I wondered whether he could be saved. My grandfather was extremely ill and had been in and out of the hospital several times.

The first time he had triple bypass, as he had suffered cardiac arrests, there was nothing else that could be done at that time. My grandfather spent several weeks in the intensive care until he was well enough to come home.

He recovered from heart surgery. He was admitted into the hospital because this time it was to go into the main arteries inside his neck, to flush out the arteries due to cholesterol build up with plaque.

Once again, Grandfather stayed a couple of weeks recovering in the ICU. Although Grandfather was weak, he was not too weak to stop molesting me or his daughter, Rosie.

During the time, my mother and step-grandmother Smith both felt traumatized and extremely exhausted, taking twelve-hour shifts caring for my grandfather.

Four months he was being homebound and cared medically at his home. Grandfather started to complain that both his legs were swollen and painful. Grandfather was barely able to stand on his legs. When he walked for a few feet, he would fall into a chair or couch, saying, "My legs hurt so bad!"

My step-grandmother called my grandfather's doctors, requesting for advice to help relieve my grandfather's throbbing, and my grandfather's doctor's advice was to bring my grandfather back to the hospital; and the heart specialist will admit, take, and strip grandfather's veins from his legs and then replace the veins inside my grandfather's heart, and with the swift hand gesture, he said, "I am not going to the hospital and get put through the same operation I had six months ago!"

My grandfather remained home. Grandfather suffered with pain and agony. I was not able to feel sorry for him. I *wanted* him to suffer, to feel as much pain as possible. I begged *God* to forgive my words toward my grandfather's suffering.

My step-grandmother explained to my mother, "If your father does not receive medical attention in the next few days, he would die from gangrene. His legs will be amputated. The survival of his living is very low."

My grandfather became worse. Both my mother and step-grandmother took my grandfather to the hospital.

He fought to keep both his limbs. It was no longer an issue to keep his legs. My grandfather was dying slowly, always in pain.

The first couple of days I visited my grandfather in the hospital, my mother and my grandfather would be sitting across from each other. They would whisper, keeping their secrets between each other. The last night before my grandfather's death, my mother sat with him on the hospital bed. My grandfather appeared tired, empty, and there was no color in his face or his eyes.

My mother handed my grandfather a silver-dollar belt buckle. Mother headed to the nurses' station. Yet somehow, my grandfather followed my mother to the nurses' station. He joked, and laughter filled the hallway of ICU. As both my grandfather and mother walked back to grandfather's hospital room, he patted my mother's butt, not as a father, but as a lover. I knew this was a gesture not of a father but the molester. I remembered this so clearly. *Grandfather died tonight!*

The Lord is my shepherd; I shall not want. He maketh me to lie down in green pastures; he leadeth me beside the still waters. He restoreth my soul; he leadeth me in the paths of righteousness for his name's sake. Yea, though I walk through the valley of the shadow of death, I will fear no evil: for thou art with me; thy rod and thy staff they comfort me. Thou preparest a table before me in the presence of mine enemies; thou anointest my head with oil; my cup runneth over. Surely, goodness and mercy shall follow me all the days of my life; and I will dwell in the house of the Lord forever.

23rd Psalm

Chapter Thirteen

GRANDFATHER'S SECRET

I raised my gaze toward my mother, who was seated next to my step-grandmother. (She is the fourth wife to my grandfather, Merton "Bud" Smith.)

My mother sat staring with despair, an expression of anguish. My mother was seated on one side of the gravesite, while the rest of the family members sat on the other side, facing mother. My half uncles and half aunts sat with their mothers, several wives of Grandfather.

The cold wind swiped through tree branches. The barren branches tried to reach upward to the dark-gray skies. The *heavens* opened up with crackling thunder, aided by the lightening tearing over the looming clouds.

Lowering my eyes, my attention focused on the freshly mound of shoveled dirt covered with outdoor plastic green carpet.

I despised my grandfather! Only a couple of weeks before his death, my grandfather visited my parent's home uninvited. Grandfather was aware that the one home was *me, only me*! I was powerless from his attacks and assaults on my bruised body. I *no longer* had to keep grandfather's secret!

Standing motionless at grandfather's coffin, inside my mind, inside my thoughts, I was *dancing*. I was dancing *"Irish Jig." The bastard was finally dead!*

I was so *relieved* I never have to encounter grandfather's stale alcohol breath. The feel of his callous hands pawing my clothes off my damaged body. I will never see his *evil* dark, black piercing eyes staring and boring into my naked soul. Tears I shed are happy ones. I was freed from the tormented memories of my grandfather' secrets.

No one believed my Aunt Rosie when she accused her father, my grandfather (Merton Bud Smith), of incest. He denied, denied, and continued to deny Aunt Rosie's cries of *rape*!

Aunt Rosie was born into my grandfather's third marriage with Dolores (Dee Dee). They married and settled in Colorado Springs, Colorado.

During one of grandfather's visits to see his children after the divorce from Dolores, Rosie was assaulted from her father (Merton

Bud Smith). Rosie told her mother (Dolores) about rape. Dolores called my grandfather's fourth wife, Christina Smith.

Either Christina could or wouldn't believe Rosie, and Rosie was blamed for the rape. The story became that Rosie was raped or agreed to have sex with a neighborhood boy. Rosie was labeled and dimed a liar.

My mother and step-grandmother, Christina, along with Rosie's siblings from Dolores, discredited Rosie's claims of sexual assault. Everyone circled their wagons around my grandfather, protecting the *evil bastard*. No one protected Rosie or me.

Of course, I realized from past history (Rosie), my sexual abuse between me and my grandfather would also be discredited.

"Rosie is lying. Rosie will and do anything to cause problems!" My grandfather acted like the injured innocent victim.

"*Who* will believe *me?*" I questioned myself into silence.

"*No one* cares!" I heard these words from my lips, also from Rosie's too.

The first time my grandfather molested me, it was on August 20, 1977, a day before my thirteen birthday.

My mother and step-grandmother were both at work. I am not sure where Mark was. I just know I was the only one home—*alone!*

My grandfather knocked loudly on the iron security door. At first, I did not hear the pounding on the front door. I was vacuuming. Grandfather continued pushing the doorbell until I opened the front door for him.

Grandfather was laughing.

"You hard of hearing, *girl?*"

His smile turned into an ugly snare. He smelled of foul, spoiled beer. His opened shirt was stained of sweat and spilled beer. His beer belly showed from the unbuttoned shirt.

He came into the house, closing both the iron security door and also the wooden front door. I heard him turning and clicking the dead-bolt locks on the doors. I realized my only chance of fleeing has been prevented with the chain connected to the door and the doorframe and door itself.

"Where is everyone?" Grandfather asked, followed with another gulp of the beer he still carried in his hand.

"Yes, am alone," I answered. It was at this time I knew that Grandfather knew I was alone. I was his cornered victim.

He winked at me as he tested the chain again on the front door.

"Just in case anyone comes home unexpected. I will be able to hear them."

Grandfather attempted to take my hand with his right hand. He was holding his beer in his left hand. I was able to struggle from his grip.

Trying to maintain my composer, I shouted "You are my grandfather. Leave me alone!" as I back further down the entryway toward the kitchen. I was praying that I would reach the back door from the kitchen.

"Oh, come on! You give your boyfriends and your brothers a taste of your sweet kisses."

Grandfather pushed me against the kitchen counter. Leaning into my face he pressed his lips hard on my mouth, prying my lips apart with his lips.

"Please! Please! Grandfather, I don't want you to do this!" I pleaded while pushing him off me.

"I'm not *good* enough for the little *princess*?" Once again, he pressed his lips onto mine, pushing his tongue through my clinched mouth.

"Don't you think your good ole' granddad deserves to taste your cherry pussy? You give your wet pussy to every Dick, Tom, and Harry."

He grabbed my hand, placing his erected penis in my hand. His penis was wet and sticky. I tried to snatch my hand away from his grip. But he held tighter and pushed my hand back and forth, stroking the disgusting penis. Keeping my hand open and holding me against him, I was not strong to get away.

"God, you're sexy. Your tits firm, and your lips are just begging for attention. I know you want me too. I see how you stare at my dick!"

He pushed his body harder into mine. The wall held me as he pulled my blouse and exposed my bare breast.

"Your grandmother—she doesn't make me hard like you do!"

His mouth was now on my breasts. He bit hard, leaving teeth marks. My nipples bled from his angry lust.

"You cannot deny your granddad from your pleasures and sweetness of your sexy pussy!" he whispered in my ear as he bit my earlobe.

I pushed him away, and he fell backward into the dining table.

"Damn, I am going to enjoy filling you up. You have spirit! Makes my dick even harder!"

Pushing him even larder into the table, he landed on the dining-table chairs. His weight crushed him further onto the chairs. I watched his eyes, slant like a serpent. His wickedness was masked with his stumbling and slurring words as he picked himself up, whispering, "I am so sorry!" He tried sounding sincere.

I did not believe one word he uttered. He was still blocking my exit from the assault. He seemed confused by my actions of retreat. His lack of words—he still had the expression of contrite.

"Yes, this is inexcusable." He moved forward, which blocked my escape.

I was hoping my grandfather was truly sorry. Then with a quick movement, he had me against the kitchen wall.

I knew my grandfather was the *devil*. The *devil* never spoke the truth.

Scrambling from his hold, I rushed into my bedroom, putting all my weight against the door.

There was *no exit.*

No place to hide…

Thud. My bedroom door flew open. Slamming my head into the dresser, I was sprawled with my stomach on the carpet. Grandfather pulled my legs to the side as he rolled me on my back. I was pushing, clawing, kicking, and screaming at this *devil!*

"I cannot think about anyone else since I saw you at the beauty pageant. You wearing that white two-piece swimsuit. Watching you strut your *ass* and moving your hips, your tits crying for me to suck you 'til you wet yourself. Well, baby, I got your message, loud and clear. *Now* you will get what you want!"

He struggled trying to keep my legs from kicking him.

"Here is my answer to your slutty pussy!"

I grabbed his hair and pushed his arms and hands away. I slapped his face, but it only increased his lust

Blood seeped from a cut in his lip from me biting him, trying to get him to stop. Licking the blood with his tongue, he said, "The more you fight, the harder and stiffer I get!"

He pushed my legs apart with his knees.

"I am about to creme myself right now!" His eyes rolled back, "Don't you want to feel Granddad's dick in your soft pussy? I know I am not the first to *fuck you*, but I sure in the *hell* will be the *best*."

With his free hand, he pulled his pants down. His knees pinned my stomach, cradling me into the carpet. His knees again pried my legs apart. He pushed my shorts and underwear to my knees, giving him more leverage to expose my lower body available for his erected penis.

"Shit! You have no clue how just looking at you. You're telling me with your eyes to screw you hard. You are begging me to give you Granddad's love. Give you the honey to fill your pussy. You are my precious and best FUCK!" His hands reached and touched my private area. "You should thank me! How lucky you are! I am going to teach my precious granddaughter how to feel and know how to screw a man!"

With a chuckle and a shove, he crammed his penis into my body. The pain was so brutal. His penis was as huge as my body would allow. The shear tearing of my body screamed for it to end. My body burned and tore into a million pieces.

Tears! *No tears, nothing would stop him!*
Screams!
Nothing stopped granddad!
Nothing!

Finally, his body shuttered. He placed his limp penis on my stomach, letting his semen squirt over my navel. My flesh felt like I was branded. The invisible brand spread over my lower and upper body, Grandfather's teeth marks burned into my breasts. More bruises appeared as Grandfather dressed himself.

"Get *up!* Clean yourself! This will teach you to prance your ass in front of *me!* You're a *whore!* You are like every other dick teaser. You deserved to be put in your place! Little *cock-teaser!*" He said, throwing my blouse at my face.

Shoving my shorts and underwear up my legs, the blood stains showed through my shorts. I could feel the cuts and tears from my lower body, and Grandfather showed no remorse. He tore my body, and *no one cared!*

Grabbing his beer from the corner of my bedroom dresser, he said, "You better tell *no one* about this! Remember what happened to Rosie? The same will happen to *you!* But even *worse!*" Grandfather waved his hand, like a dismissal to me. "Get your lazy fucking whore pussy cleaned up! Do you want more? You will have to wait 'til I get rested!

"I better get going. Don't want your mother to question why I am here." Pulling myself off the floor, he said, "Don't tell anyone about our little secret."

He wiped my midsection, where he left his brand of semen on my stomach, using my blouse as a rag. He smirked, seeing his seed over my breasts.

He laughed as he stood, looking at his trophy. He showed pride and contentment at the same time.

I was in a nightmare, standing barely clothed and feeling the physical disgust, as well as the emotional vomit, and pain.

"Just remember, you are to *blame,* my little whore! Now you will know better than to be cock-teaser. Your tight *ass!* Your pouty red lips! The way you sway your tits in front of men! You are nothing but *a bitch in heat! Nothing! Nothing more than a slut!*"

He left the bedroom, and as he walked down the hallway, he chuckled to himself. "Damn, what a tight pussy!"—his last words of blaming me; the impression that I wore like a brand on my body and my mind. I had no *self-worth!* The *blame* was all *mine!*

The *shame* belonged only to *me!*

This was the last time he would ever touch *me!*

Last time!

Grandfather now laid in the coffin, the same coffin that was being lowered into the ground!

"I hope you are in *hell!*"

"Never *rest* in *peace!*"

"You deserve *nothing!*"

"NO TEARS!"

"NOTHING!"

I shouted as loud as I could to the black coffin. My shouts were covered by the roaring thunder.

Crystal Dawn White, swimsuit and
formal attire, Beauty Pageant 1976

Vega Lake, Colorado, 1968: *right,* Crystal Dawn Gorton; *middle,* Rosie Smith (Shirley Smith—Half Sister/ Merton "Bud" Smith—Father); *left,* Mary Smith (Shirley Smith—Half Sister/Merton "Bud" Smith—Father

Far back, Harvey Leroy Gorton Jr,; *middle front,* Crystal Dawn Gorton; *far right,* Mary Smith; *right middle,* Mark Anson Gorton; *left middle,* Lester Smith; *left,* Rosie Smith

Vega Lake, Colorado, 1968: *far right,* Aunt Rosie Smith; *second from the right,* Aunt Mary Smith; Uncle Lester Smith, half brother and sister to Shirley Ann Smith-Gorton; Merton "Bud" Smith, father to Shirley and listed siblings above; *far left top,* Harvey Leroy Gorton Jr,; *front left,* Mark Anson Gorton

Thirteenth Birthday,
August 21, 1977:
Step-Grandmother
Christina Smith
and Neighbor
Hacienda Heights,
California
Grandfather Merton
"Bud" Smith.
Whitter,
California, 1976

Dogshow: Crystal
Dawn White,
Huntington Beach,
California, 1976

Mother—Shirley Ann
(Smith) Gorton-White;
Grandfather—Merton
"Bud" Smith, Hacienda
Heights, California, 1976

Crystal Dawn White
Hacienda Heights,
California 1976

Chapter Fourteen

MY FATHER IS HOME

When my father came home from the highway, he was a truck driver, driving all forty-eight states. My father was the silent *abuser*.

He owned his own rig, 18-wheeler, long hauler. He was always gone from home months at a time.

When he was home, I found peace. My bedroom was my solitude in a safe place. My mother stayed away from me while my father was home.

I was so glad when he was home. He would take my mother's attention off me. She would be the pleasant housewife for a couple of days. She would start drinking heavily and become a woman with angry insults to my father. Arguments would start. She would accuse my father of having affairs. Instead, she was the one having affairs.

I was to stay inside my bedroom until my father was in his bedroom. I was to remain silent, not to speak to him. If I had to go to school, my father must be in his bedroom.

I made sure my parent's bedroom door was shut. Thinking it was safe to leave for school, my father came out to the kitchen. I jumped, startled as he spoke to me.

"What time are you supposed to be in school?"

I froze. I dared not reply to his question. My mother stood behind my father. She motioned to stay silent. Get out of here.

"Why does she not talk with me?" my father asked my mother.

"Your daughter hates you. It is a teenager thing." Mother answered his question with a slight snarl.

My father did notice me and inquire about me. I knew, without a doubt, I would get a lashing.

I was dealt a punishment a day after our brief encounter, between my father and myself. My mother started cursing, demanding, using cruel words toward my father. He never stayed home after their arguments started.

My father was a *silent abuser* because he knew, he saw, he heard the cruel methods my mother inflicted on the children.

He remained silent!

His reasons were, a mother raised the children, and my father's job—to be a provider; to *work!*

Keep silent!

My father did not deal well with disagreements between my mother and him. My mother's mask fell off, and my father did witness the ugliness, cruelty, and evilness.

My mother portrayed the abused wife, a mistreated spouse, with her drinking of hard whiskey and a sour smell of sweating inside her clothes. She would play with dramatic emotions, expecting sympathy. She called her friends, explaining the cruel verbal and physical assault from my father's mouth and hands.

My mother's friends arrived at our house, giving Mother comfort. At this time, my mother would put on a drama play.

"Crissy, she saw the terrible way Richard treated me."

As Mother spoke, she engulfed me into her arms, brushing my hair from my forehead down my back. She would pull my hair in the back; this was her way of keeping me silent.

When my mother's friends departed, my mother was already drunk. She leaned against my legs and requested that I brush her hair. Carefully brushing her hair with tender strokes, not upsetting her, I brushed and brushed her hair until she spoke.

"Crissy, am I a good mother?"

I wanted to say, "No!" But I did not.

"Of course, you are a good mother," I replied, barely a whisper as I spoke.

My mother started falling asleep. I remained by her side.

The cycle continued throughout my childhood. *Nothing changed!* I was abandoned. My father was not my *hero!* He was the silent *abuser!*

The one time my father was home, I misjudged when he opened their bedroom door.

"Are you wearing that to school?"

I was scared my mother might overhear him. He was searching for answer. His grin turned into a frozen frown.

I was wearing the same clothes I wore a couple of days prior to when Mark tore them.

"Oh, she does not care about how she looks." my mother said as she eased herself under my father's hands that were placed on his hips.

"I make enough money. She doesn't have to dress like this."

He still was expecting an answer. I gave *none*. None! Instead, I searched into my mother's hard glaze.

"She dresses like a slob. I tried to get her to dress nicely. Take pride in herself. She does not care about her appearance. I cannot force her to.!"

My mother looked directly into my eyes. She motioned with her hands that this was not over. I betrayed her, and I would feel the punishment.

My mother slipped back into their bedroom, and as if on cue, my father followed her and closed the door.

I did try brushing my hair. It was so knotted with dry blood. The sores have not healed, and each time I pulled my brush through the tangled, matted hair, pain was unbearable.

"But once again, she'd rather look like a hobo tramp. She is a slob. No reason to even explain why or how she likes to smell."

Hearing my mother's words through the closed door, I waited to hear my father's response. There was *none*.

Mother was able to convince my father I was lazy and unclean on purpose. How do I tell my father, I have no choice but to look like and dress this way?

I hated the smirks and jeers I received from my classmates. They moved their desks far from mine. They would ask the teacher for another partner for school assignments.

I did not blame my classmates. I would've requested another partner too. At home, I was *bullied*.

At school I was *bullied too!*

The following day I wanted and waited by my parents' bedroom. I was hoping their bedroom door would open, and my father would appear.

It was worth getting a beating from my mother, which I knew I would receive.

I borrowed a pink blouse and a slim-fitted skirt to match. Thank goodness Ivy and I wore the same shoe size.

Ivy loaned me a cute, light-pink sandal shoes. I admired the young girl watching me in my mirror. I actually looked human.

Ivy gently brushed my matted hair. She tried not to pull the hair out of my scalp.

"I am so sorry. I am trying not to hurt you."

With soft strokes of the brush, Ivy managed to get most of the dried, crusty scabs out of the tangled hair.

"You look nice. This is how you should look," my father commented as he walked into the kitchen.

"You better pray your father does not have to leave tomorrow!"

My mother pressed her fingernails deep into my arm. Blood started to stain the pink blouse. With a shove, she pushed me away.

"You need to get to school. Don't want to be late, as usual," her tone was a warning of what was to be my death.

I prayed for *death!*

Once my father left to drive his 18-wheeler, I knew my punishment was going to be severe.

I was so right!

Death…did not come for *me!*

I wish it had…

Several days after my father returned to work, driving on the endless highways, my mother remained silent. She did hit, kick, and snarl cruel remarks toward my body, that I disgusted her more and more.

Every day was orchestra with making my mother's coffee. Placing her breakfast tray next to her in bed, her daily morning menu was to be carefully laid in a uniformed manner: half grapefruit, one boiled egg, with two dry slices of toast.

My next task was to brush and style her black shoulder-length hair, put her makeup, making sure that every secret of cosmetic I used were either drawn, brushed, and accented her beauty qualities. My mother's vanity—with age, I learned to skillfully make my mother look younger. The next task, I placed two outfits for my mother to choose from. The outfit she chose made her figure seem smaller and younger. The day of the Senior Prom, I carefully kept silent, not wanting to create a problem; not making one mistake! I smiled inside my head.

I did not respond to my mother's insults, not wanting to cause a flare up and excuse for my mother to stop me from attending my prom. I did every task without causing a cruel word, every chore finished without a single flaw.

I was *going to prom!*

Richard A. White standing in front of his 1974 Peterbuilt 18-wheeler, Whitter, California, August 1974

Chapter Fifteen

MARK'S RETURN HOME

Mark Anson Gorton, age six months, Cody, Wyoming

 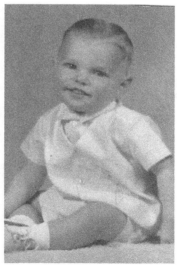

Harvey Leroy Gorton JR, four years old, Mark
Anson Gorton's first birthday, Cody, Wyoming

Richard Mark Anson White (Mark Anson Gorton),
thirteenth birthday, Hacienda Heights, Calif

Shirley Ann Smith-Gorton-White; Richard Mark Anson Gorton
White JR, age eleven years old; Hacienda Heights, California

I pulled myself back to my reality. I woke up from a trance. Feeling my body slump inward, I heard the heavy, crushing male footsteps. I knew it had to be Mark. He was approaching my bedroom door. Each footstep matched my racing heart, beating out of my chest.

"Damn it! Where the *hell* are you?" Mark's voice tore into my thoughts.

I wanted to *run*. There was nowhere to go! I could smell tobacco in the stench air, the cigarette leaving a strong smoky odor in my bedroom. Mark was searching for me. I knew exactly what he demanded from me. This has always been a part of my sexual abuse, the cycle of *hell* in my childhood.

His footsteps were closer. His fists hit and pounded the narrow walls. Mark's his fists echoed and penetrated my brain.

I was a caged animal. My thoughts screamed, "Find a place to hide myself. Maybe this time he will not find me!" Feeling the urgency, trying to conceal myself, maybe I will not get caught! *Maybe!*

Mark was two years older than me. Don't brothers protect their sisters?

Mark was my tormentor! Not my hero!

"Where are you?"

My hands trembled with fear. Mark's voice was coming through my closed bedroom door.

Where do I hide? my inner thoughts pleaded and questioned *God. Please answer me!* But my pleas were unanswered.

"You know I will find you."

Hearing Mark's voice, his tone coy, it was like cat playing with a mouse, the game of hide and seek. But this was not a child's innocent game.

"Might as will give UP!"

The bedroom door handle turned. Mark entered my bedroom. At the same moment I pried opened the bedroom-closet mirrored door. I believe I found sanctuary from this *demon* (Mark). Mark's intentions were clear. My punishment for being found was always the same.

Boxes of clothes donated by family members carpeted the closet floor. I was not allowed to wear the clothes.

I wanted to fade into the boxes, hoping the boxes were my shield and armor from the assault that I would receive without mercy from the demon! I tried not to breath! I put my balled fist in my mouth, muffling my terror! My cries! No sound escaped! I kept my whimpers from revealing my hiding place, my sobbing, keeping my body still. No movements! Be quiet!

Shallows of gulped air. *Do not breathe!* I repeated this verse inside my head.

Mark yanked open the closet door. Grabbing my hair between his fingers, I crawled further from his grasp.

Mark held onto my hair tighter. I was determined not to let him pull me from the closet. *Maybe!* Just maybe, he could not reach me. I could be *safe!* There was no place safe! *Not in my world!*

"When I call you, you better come!"

Mark's voice was heartless. He was in a rush. His tone was harsh. Although he was in a hurry, he made the time to torment and satisfy his lust.

"Please, God, *help me!*" Still another unanswered prayer.

"You could have saved yourself a lot of pain, and me a lot of trouble!"

He let my blouse fall to the floor. With a swipe with his other hand, he pulled the remaining clothes off my body.

"It is your fault the housework is not done. Everyone knows you are lazy. What an ungrateful *bitch* you are."

I tried not to react or speak from Mark's insults. He slapped my face. I was trying to remain in the closet. My mind replayed the scene. Closing my eyes, tears fell. I pictured myself in a *safe place!*

Mark forced me back to his reality. Here was the evidence of my body, soul, and mind being *raped!* Again, the scene was becoming a pinnacle.

"You know all I have to say to Mom is that you called her a *bitch!*"

I did not respond to Mark's cruel eyes, his cruel words, his cruel hands tearing, scarring, and leaving bleeding wounds on my already discarded body. There was no answer to give him. I was searching into the *abyss*, hoping the floor would devour me.

Mark was correct. My mother would believe him over me. None of my chores have been completed. Mark would lie to Mother about me. I would be *punished!*

Why did I not hide deeper inside the closet?

Why did I try to hide at all?

Why did I not try harder to prevent Mark from being angry? I should have just complied with his licentiousness.

I've been hurt worse. I could have prevented this pain.

Mark savagely attacked my body. My thoughts kept darting from one memory to the next memory. My past would appear trying to protect me the present assault. I was a shell of *nothing!*

My thoughts continued rewinding the carnality situations between myself and my brothers.

It was all my fault! I was the only one to blame! Why wasn't I submissive?

"Shut the fuck up!"

Mark slammed my head with brute force into my dresser. I was unaware that I whimpered.

The sound escaped my lips, muttering a plea, "Please *stop!*"

Mark crammed his fist into my mouth. My lips cracked from the pressure of his hand. Blood squeezed through the bottom my lip.

My mind was screaming, "Stop!" My voice was not heard.

There was nothing else you can strip from my body! Pleading in *silence! I yelled!* I imagined *both* my mother and brother heard my pleading for mercy.

Hear me!

Another push, and Mark finally released his hand from my bloody mouth.

Maneuvering himself off my torn body, he pulled his jeans up and zipped the fly, staring down at me as I grabbed my disheveled clothes scattered about me. I felt the shame. Mark was aware of the emotion I showed, and it brought an evil grin from his mouth.

"Aren't you happy to see me?" Mark asked as I tried putting the torn cloth that once was a blouse. I could not cover my bare breasts.

"You are the best piece of ass I have had in a long time."

Mark pointed the tip of his boot into my face, toward my chin. I turned my glare away from his eyes. I only saw a disgusting monster.

"You know better than to try to hide from me!" Mark's triumphant voice was laughing. I was still trying to place the tattered material over my nakedness. The blouse was not savable. The safety pins no longer held the threads together. "I missed you, *sis!*" Mark hissed. "Did you ever think of me?"

Secrets! Shame! Blame was mine to *carry!*

"You are going to wish you were dead!" my mother screamed at me for the chores not being done.

I was already *dead*. Don't you understand? I was already *dead*.

I'm alive? Why?

Mother branded me a *liar*.

I am a broken shell. I am human.

Mark hated me. He cursed me. He told me I was worthless.

He played with my *emotions*. Mark made gestures, as if he shot me in the head with a pistol.

I dared show no weakness, show *no fear!* Dared not *tell.* Mark was the reminder to *evil! Evil does exist!*

"Do you remember the last time I was here?" Mark questioned with another snarl.

"The note you wrote Mom."

I remember too well. I got a beating from my mother's belt buckle. I still have a deep scar on the back of my upper thigh.

"I warned you not to say anything about our secret. It was our private time, *our lovemaking, our secret!*" Mark's voice cracked with anger.

"I denied everything. Guess what happened?" Mark stroked my inside leg then twisted my thigh, leaving a red bruise. "The beating you *deserved!*"

Of course, I remember! The welts on my skin. I lost count of the number of lashes I received from both Mother and Mark. One of the lashes embedded Mother's belt buckle in my skin.

My mother read the note I wrote. I detailed every act of incest that both of my brothers had assaulted on me, their cruel, perverted, sickening molestation; the sexual lust and acts I had been abused with—rape, oral, and traded to other friends of Mark and Harvey, paying off their debts to someone. I was the payment.

Carrying the *shame* was enough punishment. *Not* to mother.

My mother, she was furious with me.

She said, "You are a liar!" She said, "You lied to me about this *bullshit!* You will lie to someone else. What if they believe you?"

My *secrets*. My mother's *secrets*. Mark's *secrets*. Grandfather's *secrets. Family secrets*

My mother yelled me to me, "Get you father's belt."

I handed her the buckle end. She whipped the belt around, and the buckle was at the end of the lashes I received. I felt the cold, hard buckle across my thighs. I pictured the beautiful silver rodeo trophy of a bull roping cowboy, sitting on his strong mustang horse. The buckle had Father's name engraved, "*Anson*." I admired the buckle with gold trim and silver in lay. The buckle was used as my punishment and weapon.

"Mom, you know Crystal is a liar. She is lying. I never laid a hand on her. *Never!* Crystal wants me to get in trouble! Mom, you don't believe me?"—Mark's accusations that I was lying.

Mark denied and whined to Mother, "I never laid a hand on her!"

"Even if you did have sex with your sister, she probably begged for it. Crystal needs to keep her mouth shut. Telling lies about this family."

My mother held the leather strap and swung with all her power. The buckle broke through the flesh, into the bone.

"Take those school clothes off. Not a stitch of clothes on you! Mark, hold her arms. Keep her straight. I am going to beat the lies out of *her!*"

I tried to get my hands free to cover my body. But Mark held on tightly. The buckle hit my back, shoulders, and my butt.

"Mark, turn her around. I want her to remember this!"

My mother was getting tired. I prayed the beating is over. Instead, Mother handed Mark the belt. Mark' mouth turned in a happy face. He snickered, showing his amusement as he released my wrists.

"She lied about you. You have the right to punish her. Take your revenge. Beat the lies out of her!"

I sank to the floor.

My mother pulled my crumbled body onto the couch. "Get your *ass up!*" She was pushing my upper body to lean over the couch's side.

"Tell me you are lying!" Each lash from the leather belt smashed against my skin.

Mark aimed for the flesh on my body that had not been marked with scars and bruises. Mark showed no remorse.

I kept silent. Mother expected me to say I was lying. *I am not a liar!* I would not give either my mother or brother the satisfaction of saying, "*I lied!*"

"You better tell me you are a liar. A whore. You will go to *hell* for being a liar!"

I remained quiet. In my thoughts, I was screaming at her, "Didn't you not know? I am already in *hell.*"

My mother pointed to Mark, "Do not *stop!* She better tell me the truth."

"I am not lying," I could only whisper.

"You know damn well you are lying about your brother!"

Finally, I could not handle another lash from the belt.

Keeping my eyes lowered, I whispered, "I am sorry. I will not say anything again about Mark or you."

I wanted every ounce not to recant my story or truth. I could not endure the pain.

"You better tell Mark how grateful you are to have him as your brother." With her back toward me, Mark motioned his delight in my misery. "You deserved this punishment. How lucky you are that he is so understanding." Trying not to show defeat, wiping the tears away, I stood straight, looking at them both.

"You are not sorry enough!"

She took the brown-and-orange blanket off the chair, dog hair sticking through the fabric.

"*You* are to take every piece of dog hair off this blanket."

I picked up my clothes; she slapped the clothes from my grasp.

"You will not need clothes, and if there is one piece of dog hair left on the blanket, you will be whipped again. Each hair will be worth a whip."

With a gesture of her hands, I was dismissed.

"I want you sit on the floor in the spare bedroom." My mother wiped her soiled and bloodied hands on my clothes. "You are a nasty, filthy girl. You do not deserve to sit on nice things."

The bloody belt laid over the arm of the couch. I limped around the couch. I did not want to look at this thing that had caused me so much pain.

I tried hard not to vomit, seeing the leather belt and the stains of blood smeared and sprayed on couch. The walls were splattered with my blood. I could not refrain from vomiting. I wiped the vomit from my mouth and floor with the blanket full of dog hair. It had been two days since I had water or food. I tucked the vomit inside, out of sight from my mother's view.

I was dizzy; my head felt like bricks. I felt the blood at the corners of my mouth.

Mark appeared at the bedroom door. He was instructed to make sure I followed through with the chore.

I was not allowed to fall asleep.

Darkness covered my eyes. A heavy feeling inside my head, *I fainted.*

Shaking me awake and splashing my face with water, Mark loomed over me.

"Mom is going to beat you *again*. This time, with every inch of your life!" Mark's words meant nothing to me. He lied. He showed no mercy. He made sure I would not resist him again. I was to please him.

I was his hostage. He made my life a living *hell*. He had the power; he controlled my every movement.

I had no power.

I do not know which *abuse* was worse or *damning!*

My mother's physical punishments that never ended…

Mark's brutal emotional *abuse*, along with the *sexual abuse*.

I remained *silent*.

No resistance against the sexual assaults. I was to lay absolutely still. *Not uttering* a word. No sounds passed through my lips.

As Mark scarred, bruised, and beat my skeleton body, he suffocated my screams. He penetrated my soul, body, and mind with each labored and rapid thrusts that he would demand my shame. My shadow, my life was rhythmical to his conquests.

I felt *nothing!*

Convincing myself I was the idiot, I was to blame, Mark's perverted actions were my secrets.

I could, I should, and would have. I made excuses.

Chapter Sixteen

BEGINNING TO THE END

Patrick kept his sexual origins silent. High-school students could be incredibly cruel, especially to those students that might not fit into a tight small box. Both Patrick and I did not fit in with cliques, like the jocks, cheerleaders, geeks, comedian, or drama nerds.

We followed to our own beat of the drum. Current fashions or popular music did not exist in our world.

Patrick hid from his sexuality, and I hid from view.

Keeping secrets? Secrets that were not mine to keep.

We were high-school students, plowing through different stages of teenage levels, each milestone achievement.

Normal! What is *normal?* Such a broad word. *Yet* so many meanings from birth to death, and this word described every stage of a person's life

Thank goodness there were abnormal human beings in the human race. Otherwise, we would still be in the caveman thinking. There would be no fire, round wheel, and we would use caveman vocal mannerisms. Me man, you woman. Male species clubbed the female with a tree limb. He would drag the female species into the caves. Some things have not truly changed. Still, have cliques, snubbed persons not fitting into that tight, closed, bowed box.

Fear! Terror! was the source of domination and power control.

I realized how my mother used these same tackle maneuvers to keep me a prisoner inside her web of *hate*.

I also learned a tool: *survival!*

I learned to keep secrets. I kept Patrick's secret. I felt the turmoil and fear he was facing. Patrick wished to be accepted.

Fear, cruel finger-pointing classmates talked under their breath, whispered behind school books; physical torments. *Normal!* Patrick and I both are *normal!* School students made judgment inquisitions. Maintaining the thought process, if you were a person who was not *normal*, you must be exterminated or exiled.

Therefore, both Patrick and I continued keeping our lies, being normal. Patrick did not allow others to know his secret. I did not reveal nor speak the awful truth about secrets behind the closed doors.

Patrick and I kept our bond to each other.

Patrick had the heart of a giant and a loving soul.

Our connection was held together by our secrets. We remained silent.

We were keeping questions unanswered. We wanted to stay hidden.

Both Patrick and I discussed the prom. We hatched a plan that he would be my prom date. I just needed to plant the seed into my mother's mind. I told my mother I did not want to go to prom, nor did I want Patrick to be my escort to the prom.

My mother took the bait. Mother wanted family members to believe I was living the *normal* teenage girl's dream.

Of course, there were hurdles that I had jump over before I was given permission to go to prom.

I had to buy the prom dress and tickets, not to forget the limo rental fees too.

My mother's live-in boyfriend came to my aide. He was renting a bedroom from my parents. Truth, Johnny was my mother's lover while my father was driving long-haul freight through the lower forty-eight states. Which meant he was absent at least two months at a time. But when he did come home, it was maybe three to seven days at a time. My mother would act loving for the first couple of days that my dad came home off the road. Mother pushed Dad to get back on the road and drive his 18-wheeler and *make money*. My mother started arguments with my father so he would leave.

Johnny witnessed the abuse that I received. He stayed silent.

"I am afraid if I disagree with your mother about the harsh treatment, she would show you I could no longer live here." This statement was repeated several times through the years.

"Why don't you take my son, Steve, to the prom? Your mother will not ever know, and I will purchase your prom dress, tickets, and half of the rental for the limo."

Johnny watched from the hallway as my mother told me the details that I would need to go to prom.

For several weeks my mother tried to block me from prom. Yet I kept my focus on the prize (Senior Prom).

"I do not know how you are going to go to prom. You have no dress, no money to pay for the ticket. *Guess* you're not going!" She crinkled her nose and with a swift movement of her hand. I cringed and prepared myself for another blow of her fist.

"Silly girl. I do not need to hit you. You're already feeling miserable." Mother had an evil laugh as she pushed me aside.

Johnny was sitting in the dining room, and I caught a glimpse of his wink to me. Yes, he was on my side.

Who would have thought this prom meant this much to me?

It was a goal post that I wanted to leap over.

My fairytale night finally arrived!

Patrick and I felt the confidence to be one of the cool kids, accepted by our peers.

I was able to climb another milestone to adulthood.

Patrick would not be sneered at. He would be envied for escorting a senior to the prom. We could hardly contain our excitement inside the limo. Our fairytale began flawlessly. Together we felt untouchable.

We held hands and gossiped among ourselves. Ivy sat with her prom date across from me, Patrick, and Steve (Johnny's son).

The hour-and-half drive to the Bonaventure Hotel in Los Angeles felt like seconds to get to our destination.

I squeezed Patrick's hand and leaned toward him and said, "You will have a great night. Enjoy every moment. I promise, you will have a precious memory from tonight. No one will ask you, ever again, if you are *gay!*"

Patrick squeezed my hand in acknowledgement that he felt the same way too.

"We may be misfits, but I am happy that you are my partner of the misfits club." I smiled at his huge hands engulfing my small hands.

"Someday I will hold my head up high and announce to the world, '*Yes, I am gay!*'"

He turned his attention on the cars that passed us on the freeway. The dark shadows looming from the street lights were a reminder of the dark life I was to return to at home.

"This is not the day to be gloomy. It is a lovely night," Patrick whispered.

"Pinch me. I am not sure if I am dreaming, or is this really happening!" I laughed, watching the beautifully dressed Ivy. The handsome young men dressed in tuxedo, bow, and cover bun.

Nope. This was not a dream. I pinched myself for reassurance.

I thought about the pain and tears I had endured this week, trying to anticipate my mother's every movement.

I walked on eggshells since my mother gave her consent. I was so afraid I would give mother a reason or chance to recall her kindness of allowing to participate in the rites of senior milestones. If she had a clue that I was happy inside, she would have dashed the whole idea of prom. Anytime I felt the emotion of joy, or even looked happy, she would remove that emotion away real fast.

I prayed for the right to go to prom, the passage that most senior classmates dreamed of, then walking down the senior graduation. These few milestones in a young person's life into adulthood, I felt honored to be in.

Closure of school years were right around the next corner.

My adulthood was only a few months away.

Staring out into the darkened sky, stars peered into the limo from above. My thoughts were reminded to earlier today.

Wow! I almost blew it!

I raced home from the school bus, trying to get all the chores written on the list that Mother hung on the refrigerator. Every day Mother would leave a list of chores to finished before her…arrival home after work.

Sometimes Mother wanted to trick me. She would hide the chore list. It would take several precious minutes to search for the chore list.

Sometimes I was not able to locate the chore list. I tried to remember what my mother usually wrote on her lists. I never failed. I forgot a chore. Mother wrote down on her list. Of course, it was my fault for completing my chores. I did not follow her directions and failed to complete all the tasks.

For instance, I ironed Mother's clothes. I made sure the clothes were wrinkle-free. My mother was in one of her rages. She took the ironed garment. My mother balled the garment and threw it in a corner of room. I picked up the clothes off the floor, and Mother would yank it out of my arms. With her shoes, she twisted and left a shoe print and tear. I would be beat with iron cord, or worse, the silver face of the iron swinging into my legs, arms, and back.

I tried to cover the bruises with a long-sleeve shirt.

My legs would be covered with red lashes and deep bruises. I wore long pants to conceal the scars.

On special occasions, my mother loved to play cat-and-mouse game. She would take the chore list with her to work. She would arrive home, announce with a glee, "*Oh*, here is the list." She would take list it out of her purse.

She would smile with a smirk and quiz me, "Well, did you do all the chores?" My mother knew I was unable to follow the list. I did not have it to follow.

"No, I could not find the list. Did you put one out for me?" I asked, keeping my eyes lowered to the floor.

"Are you questioning me? YES! I LEFT YOU A LIST, YOU TWIT!"

I watched Mother take the chore list out of her purse and place it inside the kitchen drawer.

Quickly Mother pulled my tangled hair with her fist and said, "You are a lazy bitch. Aren't you?" Mother opened the drawer, removing the hidden list. "Well, lookee here, the missing list." Mother crumbled the chore list and crammed the paper into my mouth. "Here! Eat the whole list. Just like a piggy. Eat every piece of it. Swallow all!"

My mother dug her fingernails into my arm underneath, leaving bruises. Unseen under the forearm, my mother twisted her fingernails deeper and deeper into my flesh.

"Chew on this like a piggy. You must *love* it when I get *mad!* Why else do you get me angry? Swallow it. Every word, every piece. Better not let any piece fall out of your lying mouth!"

Mother stood watching me chew every last piece of paper until none was left inside my mouth. In my mind, I fantasized I was a secret agent, eating the chore list as if I was eating a mission. I was keeping my mission from falling into the wrong hands. *Meanwhile,* my mother continued to watch for another reason—to slap, kick, and pull my flesh. I didn't give her any reason.

She stalked off with a huff, "Will you better not question me again." As an afterthought, my mother turned back, facing my cowardly body, looking for an excuse to torment me.

Finding a fault for my ill-treatment from my mother's actions, she said, "You should have called me. Stop looking like I hurt you. You are such a *drama queen!*"

With a brush of her hand, I jilted to block a hit from my mother.

My throat was raw from the jagged edges of the staples that pierced the top of my mouth. *Do not shed tears! Show no emotions!*

My mother continued ratting about what a disgusting vomit I was. I reminded myself not to gag. But I did gag. My mother's attention turned toward me. My mother's slap impacted my jaw to shake. Still I remained unemotional, my eyes lingered on the floor. Since I did not say or show arguments to my mother, she became a bored and sighed. Her wedding rings left an impression on my chin. My mother smirked at the blood dripping from both jaw and lips.

"I am sorry, Mother. *I promise* to do better next time. *I promise never let it happen again. I promise.*" Keeping my arms to my side, I *showed no emotions*. My eyes swelled with tears. "*Do not show tears!*" I repeated this over and over as she swayed into her bedroom.

I learned not to whine, show no pain. Otherwise, my mother would again smack, kick, and push me. My mother would find any object to use to hit me within arm's distance. To defuse the situation, I had to remain in a cowardly stance. Remain absolute silent. No quick movements. I was my mother's pry. She received the victory of the spoils. *I showed no emotions!*

This did not always work either. When my mother was in a terrible mood, it did not matter *what, how, or why* I was the target.

"You want sympathy? You deserve nothing from me! You are the reason why my life is messed up. You are only another mouth to feed. Look at my body, you did this to me! You and your brothers. You are worthless, not even worth looking at! You make me sick. Nothing but a piece of trash. What, you have nothing to say?"

Her outbreaks of cruelty unusual happened when my father left to get peace and solace from the empty truck with eighteen wheels guiding his abrupt escape from the wicked witch. My mother could say many terrible, cruel words with *no remorse*. My father felt the sting of my mother's spilling *evilness* toward my father.

"I wish I succeeded in aborting you. Did you know I took a pill to get rid of you while I was three months pregnant? Obviously, you did not flush down the toilet." My mother's eyes showed agitation toward me.

"You should have drowned, not JR It is your fault he is dead. You make up stories about JR, and JR left to stay with Harvey. My precious angel, JR You are a nasty whore slut!"

Mother's drinking became endless, and Mother continued to attack my body. My mother loved *drama*, her crocodile tears spilling into her sour and whiskey drink. *Yes*, mother was correct. I created a horrific life for her. Every disgusting detail of my miserable life, my every existence, was all my fault.

Mother was right. I should have been the child to die. *Not* JR. JR was no longer in pain anymore. He did fear my mother's assaults on his body, mind, and soul. Our mother imprinted scars on our bodies. I tried to feel what JR felt as he took his last breath. "Did you find solace, peace, and with your last inhale of breath?" I asked JR in my thoughts. "Did you finally feel peace among the guardian angels? Will my last thoughts before death also be *peace* for *me*?"

I questioned my own sanity. Why? *Why*, God, *did I stay* alive? *Can you not see the* pain*, the sadness in my heart? My soul and mind damaged with every strike of anger from my mother's hands?*

My life meant nothing to my mother. Did it mean anything to *God*?

As if hearing my thoughts, I told myself, "You are *alive!* You *fight* to stay that way. *Alive!* Never give *in*." My life meant nothing to my mother, but it meant *everything to me!*

Pulling my thoughts back into the present, I had enough playing recorder in my brain, remembering the injustice of my mother's life. The invisible tears, no moister in the tears she pretended to shed.

Her only emotion was of *hate*. The harsh words that spilled from her evil mouth. The baby that was a product of disdain into her life.

I focused on my chores, chores I had not been able to complete. *Shit!* Where was that *damn* list?

I did not want anything to go wrong today. I knew my mother wanted to toy with me, the cat-and-mouse game.

I told myself, "Think what is usually on the list and just do it."

I vacuumed the entire house, moved rugs and furniture. There have been few occasions my mother had me use the broom, sweeping the fur, dirt and miscellas off the carpet. I used the yard rake to pull the carpet, leaving no signs of footprints, or any evidence that someone walked on this room. When my mother noticed I missed anything on the carpet, I was to use the tiny hand broom, and on my hand and knees I swept the entire room.

My mother would pull my ears and push me into the carpet where footprints remained imprinted on the carpet. My mother smashed my face and rubbed my nose into the fabric, leaving rug burns. My mother's last assault on me, she placed her knees into my back and jumped on and off my lower back. My mother wanted total power and control.

"What do you see, my little piggy? I will tell you what I see. I see your fucking footprints. *Redo* it again until I think it is *done right! Now!*

My mother pushed me abruptly into the carpet. I stayed in a fetal position, keeping myself still.

"I need to get the dirty laundry finished!" In a frantic jump, I searched for the discarded clothes.

"I better wash the clothes by hand and hang them dry in the garage. Since it has been raining most of the day." I mentally went down the imaginary chore list. "I better iron her clothes that she will wear for work tomorrow."

If there were wrinkles after I had ironed the garments, I knew she would make me start over and over again.

"Now I need to get the dusting done. I made sure all the lamps and figurines are moved, dusted, and placed everything exactly were Mother had put them."

Mother took her fingers and wiped the tables and lamps, making sure I dusted every nick and corner. If I left film from the polish or did not wipe the articles to her standards, my mother would force me to continue wiping the items over and over. Mother would find flaws in my house chores, no matter how hard I tried to complete a task. Mother used these chores as another excuse to punish me. I doubled and tripled, making sure my chores were done completely.

4:30 PM. The house phone was ringing. I sprinted into the kitchen. The house phone was attached on the wall between the kitchen and dining room.

Damn it! I missed the phone. Mother was going to be so mad. *Now!* Mother will have an excuse because I didn't catch the phone ring by the third ring. My heart pounded into my throat. Memories flooded my mind. Tears fell uncontrollably.

Couple of weeks ago, my mother questioned me, "Can you hear the phone *now?*"

Blood foamed through my gums and swollen lips with each blow I received from the phone receiver. Mother used the phone as a weapon on my skull. I wiped my already-soiled blouse to catch blood from dripping on the floor.

"Yes, I hear you," I mumbled. I dared not look into her face I lowered my arm, as if in submission.

"What! You want to hit me?" Another blow to my upper arm, I blocked the receiver front hitting my head, the next hit.

"Maybe I should call the police and explain how this *slut* of a daughter tried and did hit me!"

Mother was shaking the phone receiver in front of her face. She went to the wall and began dialing the phone number.

"No, I did not try to hit you, Mother." I pushed my body inward against the wall.

"Hell you didn't. You want to go to juvenile hall? With other kids, maybe get raped or lost into the child services protection? I bet you will like that! Little whore." I remained silent.

"Why, can't you answer me? Worthless piece of *shit!* I bet you will hear the phone *now!*"

After this incident, it took weeks for the bruising and lumps to fade away. My hearing was white noise with static and humming. I prayed that I did not get another beating, especially not *today.*

Mother was content with my reply, "No, Mother. I do not want leave you. I love you."

Staring at the floor was the image of wiping my blood from the phone receiver.

"No, Mother. I do not want you to leave. I do not want to leave you either. *I love you!*"

I told myself, "*I will survive!*"

I scampered through the house, making sure I finished my chores. I prayed and prayed for my *death…*

Last couple of days…*I wanted to die!*

My memory of the senior prom was both my happiness and agony.

I would never allow my mother to take away or shatter my memory. *Never!*

Chapter Seventeen

PROM NIGHT

The arrangement we made with the limo service was that the driver would pick me and Patrick at my house since I had to dress at Ivy's house because our plans changed.

Johnny's son, Steve, met us at Ivy's home.

Ivy's mother was informed why I had two dates to the prom.

"Only you would get away with two dates." Patrick was smiling and joking.

"Crystal, I told Mother about how terrible your mother is!"

Ivy was putting the finishing touches to her beautiful black hair.

"Why? I asked you not to tell anyone!"

I did not want Ivy's mother to show pity or the need to hug me. I wanted tonight to remain happy and feel the joy of no fear.

"I could not keep silent anymore. I am sorry."

"It's okay. Please let's not talk about my mother. I want enjoy our senior prom."

Ivy and I have a sister bond. Ivy was the only one I trusted or spoke to about the violence in my home. I am so glad and thankful that Ivy did tell her about my mother. Ivy's mother saved my life. I believe this with all my being!

"Let's have fun. Tonight is our night."

I placed my arm through both Patrick's and Steve's arm. We skipped to the limo. Our fairytale night has begun. Midnight the limo would turn into a pumpkin.

All of us laughed, danced, and enjoyed a wonderful dinner at the senior prom.

The Cinderella clock struck midnight.

Where was the limo? And the driver?

After the ballroom closed down, we sat at the curb of the hotel entrance, waiting for the limo to gather all of *us* and take us home.

"Crystal, what time is the limo supposed to be back?" Patrick asked.

Ivy and I were shaking from the cool breeze. Our gallant escorts removed their tuxedo jackets and placed the jackets over our shoulders against the chill.

"The driver was to be here by midnight," I answered.

We watched other prom guests leave the empty ballroom.

"I am going to call the limo service. Stay put. I'll be right back. Just need to use the front desk's phone."

I felt desperate agony. My heart fell to the pit of my stomach.

The front desk clerk searched for the limo-service phone number and dialed the number.

"Hello. My name is Crystal White. The limo driver has not arrived to pick us up at the Bonaventure Hotel. Yes, we are the seniors from the prom." I wasn't expecting a reply that the limo dispatched told me.

"Miss White, your mother, Shirley White, made arrangements for the driver to pick your mother with two additional guests from the residence to the restaurant the Cliff House in Riverside."

Oh *my god!* My mother made a beautiful night into a horrible nightmare.

"What time will the limo driver be able to pick us up?" My stomach turned into stone.

"Since we are discussing the situation with you, the driver notified me using a two-way the radio. He is about two to three hours from retrieving you and the other student in your party."

"Thank you," I mumbled to both the front desk clerk and limo dispatch.

"Miss, why don't you and friends stay inside by the fireplace in the sitting-room area? You will all be safe and kept warm 'til your ride arrives." The clerk gave a smiling and encouraging look.

"Thank you," I said, hanging my shoulders and head down, not wanting anyone to see my tears. I knew my nightmare has not even started yet.

A wrecking ball would feel better in the head than having to tell the others that they needed to call their parents to explain our limo driver was delayed. They should be home between 4:00 and 5:00 AM.

I explained the situation to Ivy, Ivy's escort, and Patrick. My excuse was that my mother, the schedule time, that the prom was over at midnight. I could tell neither Ivy or Patrick believed my story. They could read through the lines. This was no accident.

"Ivy, I am so sorry." Ivy sad eyes stared at my own teary eyes. Ivy was aware that my night would be a *hell night*! A horror night when I get home.

The limo driver arrived at the Bonaventure Hotel around 2:30 AM. Our driver in the limo was very quiet. My head throbbed with the knowledge that my hour of doom was around corner.

There was no laughter or gossiping between the prom guests. Each of us tried to find ways to explain to their parents for the delay or tardiness from the senior prom.

"Tell the truth," I answered their question. "Please do not worry. I will be *fine!*" I didn't believe this lie.

Patrick squeezed my hand and gave me a kiss on the cheek. He walked into his house.

My date, Steve, was dropped at Denny's restaurant. One of Steve's friends picked him from there. Didn't want my mother to see Steve.

Finally, I was dropped off at my home. I crawled over the vacant seats.

"Are you aware this an extra charge of $75 due upon the dropping you off? The extra charge is for the pick-up and drop off of your mother and her two guests."

At this time, Johnny headed to his car, getting ready to go to work.

"Johnny!" I rushed to him before he unlocked the car door. "I need another $75 to pay for the limo. Mother took her and two friends out last night. I owe another $75. What am I going to do?" I was so terrified that Mother would find out about taking Steve to prom. Johnny seemed baffled.

"What are you talking about?" Johnny put his green lunch box on the passenger seat.

"Johnny, Mother called the limo service. Mother and her two friends to drive them to and from the Cliff House restaurant."

"Are you serious?" Johnny questioned me.

"Yes, I have to pay *now!*"

I could not stop shaking from fear and the burden of begging Johnny to help me.

"I will take care of it. Get inside. Your mother is asleep. Hurry, change your clothes so your mother will not know what time you got home."

Johnny wiped my black mascara from my runny face with his clean gray shirt. He pulled his wallet from his jeans.

"Here is a hundred, for your tip and extra guests." Johnny handed the driver a hundred bill.

I opened the front door quickly and slipped into my bedroom. *I hope Patrick and Ivy did not get into much trouble.* My mind was racing through the night filled with every motion possible.

"Please, God! Do not let Patrick or Ivy get into trouble," I prayed while I removed my fairytale dress off and into a garment bag.

My thoughts were about a happy time and place. I went to sleep next to my mother's side of the bed on the floor.

I had no clue that *hell* would be better than what I was going to endure the following morning and the next forty-eight hours. This was the *beginning* to the *end*. My life was transparent to my guardian angel. I was powerless, and I had no control.

I had gained survival instincts, which helped fulfilled my destiny. *I prayed for death!*

Crystal Dawn White and Patrick, 1982 Senior prom

My mother with her two friends from the ranch, where my parents kept their horses. The reason the limo driver was detained: he picked up and dropped off my mother and her guests to and from the restaurant.

Chapter Eighteen

BOXING MATCH

I slept through the telephone rings. It started to ring again. Glazing at the clock, it was 4:30 PM. I was able to pick up the receiver as the last ring echoed through the house. I knew it was my mother.

"Damn it," I could hear her voice angry at the empty rings.

I found my mother's work number on a torn piece of paper tucked against the phone attached on the kitchen wall. I prayed my mother was assisting customers at the register. Usually, when my mother was helping customers, my mother was pleasant. "*Please, please!* Answer the phone, Mother."

Let Mother be busy. Jack answered the phone, "House of Cutlery, Jack speaking. How may I assist you?"

Jack had been employed at the House of Cutlery for ages, at least twenty years before my mother was hired.

"Jack, is my mother busy?" I whispered with a shaking, trembling voice.

"Why, no, honey." He sounded shocked at my question. "I sent your mother home early. Since we are not busy. Your mother said you were feeling ill. Probably the flu or a virus. Are you feeling better?" Jack seemed really concerned.

"I think I have the flu," I replied. "I started feeling ill at school. I left early with a slight fever." I was feeling really sick *now!*

"I hope you feel better soon," Jack's reply was in a joking tone.

"Thank you, Jack."

My stomach was queasy. I should have asked Jack when my mother had left work. That would have allowed me time to run and hide.

I placed the receiver into the phone cradle as my mother's car pulled into the driveway. Barely put in park, my mother darted out of the driver's seat. Slamming the car door shut, Mother's high heels pounded on the cement toward the front door. Her shoes sounded like a machine gun, rapid firing of bullets, fast and faster with each shoe pounding with my heartbeat.

"Get your *ass* in here right *now!*"

I wanted to rush past her, out of the front door, down the driveway. I would be out of her reach. My mother cornered me against the entryway, blocking my escape to *freedom!* A loud *bang!* The front door slammed *shut!*

I was a mouse being toyed with as the cat aimed for a final kill. My mother's claws became daggers, slicing into my arm.

"Thought you could run away from *me?*"

I remained silent, no reply needed.

"You going to wish you were never born!"

My mother's voice hissed into the air. I felt her breath. The venom of her cruel words no longer hurt me.

"I wish I wasn't born too," I mumbled beneath my breath.

Funny! My mother's words did not hurt my heart or soul. "How are you going to hurt or mangle me, dear mother?" My thoughts raced. "Why didn't I just *shut up?*" I questioned my inner self. I was only making my mother angrier. As if answering my silent question, Mother grabbed my hair with every ounce of strength she possessed. Mother pulled my body into the entryway and pushed my face smacked into the floor tile.

"This is the day you will meet your maker. *God* knows you are worthless piece of *shit.* Shit, I wipe off the bottom of my shoes!" My mother spat these cruel words with hatred. "You will *die! No one! No one* will care!" "*God,* I am here! *God, hear me!*"

No response. The crashing of my mother's fists landed on my back, my head, everywhere my mother wanted to inflict *pain.*

I fainted circled blackness cloud. Blood dripped down my face; blood splattered on the tile and walls.

My mother continued hitting, kicking, and slapping me. A gulf of darkness became the relief from the pain. Excruciating *pain.*

When did Mother change her high heels? My mother was wearing cowboy boots! How long have I been passed out? I heard my voice; it sounded distant from my body. The cowboy boots heel smashed my ribcage. My shoulders felt like mush. My head pounded with every hit, kick, and push. My voice, I screamed, and no sound came out. I was like a rag doll.

"Stop!" I begged my mother to stop.

My screams filled the house. *Please stop!* My mother hit me in my stomach, which made me roll off the entry tile, onto the living-room carpet. Mother pulled me with my shirt collar and hair back onto the tile. Screams came from me! With each blow from mother's fist, kick, or hair pulling, another scream pierced through my throat and lips.

"*Please, please stop!*" I begged Mother to *end* this torture from the outside to the inside of my body.

"I explained to Patrick's father. He must be extremely proud of his son. The reason the limo driver was late returning everyone home, at the curfew time agreed upon, because you and Patrick were fucking inside the limo. My dear, little slut, How you have made Patrick's father truly proud with his bastard son. Bravo!"

My mother giggled and snickered, enjoying the sweet conversation she and Patrick's father discussed. My mother straddled onto my back, spurring her heels into my ribcage. And with a *yeehaw*, she kicked, guiding me to carry her like a saddled horse. The kicking and pulling on my hair was no match to the punches my mother slaughtered my stomach with.

"I told Ivy's mother the same reason I told Patrick's father. Also said I was very disappointed with my daughter's behavior." I did not want to hear any more, but Mother was extremely proud of herself. "This whole thing would be dealt with." I lost conscience and did not hear the rest of gleeful voice.

"My little *Crissy!* How I do care about your whore and slut reputation?" My mother's laughter was dark and evil.

The sound of the doorbell ringing brought me back to the present. My brain was filled with fog, my body bruised and bloody. Patrick and Ivy stopped ringing the doorbell and pounded relentlessly.

"Answer the door, Mrs. White.!" Patrick was yelling and banging his fist against the door. Each hit vibrated through the tile.

"Open this door right now!" Ivy's voice was rough, commanding. "The cops are on their way. Open the door!"

My mother pushed my body against the doorframe, unseen between the crack of the opening.

"What do you want?" my mother hissed through the opening. I could see the shadow of Ivy's shape. "You have no reason to be here. Get off my porch, or I will tell the police you are trespassing!" My mother's voice was not at all concerned about the police showing up. She would sweettalk her way out of any situation.

"Go home *now!* If your parents need any more information about last night, I will be more than happy to explain again how nice my lovely daughter was to you, Patrick."

I could hear Patrick; he was trying everything possible to get me out of there.

"I said to leave. I *mean walk away!*" My mother's words were loud and shrieking shrill.

I listened to Patrick's and Ivy's footsteps retreating. Patrick's truck was loud. Patrick gunned the engine as he backed his vehicle, backing onto the main street.

My mother watched Patrick drive his truck down the street. This gave me a chance to pick myself off the floor, and I rushed past my mother. I was able to push Mother out of the front door entryway. I was running with a limp and holding my right arm. My arm felt as if it was out of its socket. I managed to get across the street. Patrick saw me in his rearview mirror, waving him down to *stop* and turn around to get me.

I could hear Mother's long-stride cowboy boots behind me. I felt the blood rushing out of my head. My mother was yelling at me to "STOP!"

Mother screamed, "Patrick hit *her!*"

The neighbors closed their front doors and remained invisible as my mother continued screaming at the top her lungs.

"Get in the house, *Crissy!* You should be sitting down. Especially after Patrick hitting you!"

Mother closed the door as her last sentence was yelled for the neighbors to hear and witness Mother's display of affection and drama. I stopped in my tracks. My mother spun the entire episode was Patrick's fault.

"Patrick, you and Ivy go on home. I will be fine." I gave both Ivy and Patrick a half smile. "It will be okay." I wanted them safe while my mother was spinning her web of lies, trying to cover her outbursts.

My back cringed, the lashes from my mother's assault never wavered. "This is what I deserved!" My thoughts were pleading for this to *end*.

Biting my lips, I tried to stay silent, not giving my mother satisfaction of seeing the hurt and pain she delivered upon my broken spirit and skin. Mother's enthusiasm of watching me slowly disappear into the floor.

"You are a waste of breath!"

Mother said with one last kick into my ribs, "I do not even know why you were even born!" her distained voice trailing after her. Mother left me on the tile floor curled in a fetus position. "You were not even supposed to be born."

I didn't hear anything after my mother went into her bedroom. *Silence, only silence!* My ears were ringing, my heart in tatters, my body scattered and splattered on the floor, walls and my bloodstains between the grout in the tile flooring.

"Why did you have *me*?" I spoke loudly. I did care if Mother heard me.

I had nothing to lose, not *now*. "God, answer me, *please* answer me! Why am I here?" I repeated this question over and over. My mother talked loudly so I would hear her."

"I tried to abort you. But here you are. The disgusting girl, child, or whatever you are. *I hate you!*"

I searched for a leverage to pick myself off the floor. I focused on the doorknob; it was the closest door I could pull my body upward. The white paint on the bathroom door stained with splatters of blood and raw skin. Each time my mother raised her arm to deliver another hit from the belt, blood would be swung and laid on the door, floor, and tile.

The moment my mother was out of sight, I bolted for the door. Every inch of my body ached.

"Kris, *over here!* Behind the car!" Ivy voice was shaking.

"What are you doing here?" I whispered, concealing from my mother. I was relieved that they stuck around. My emotions were rattled. "I need to get you guys out of here!" I was on my knees, hiding myself behind the car too. "You guys have to leave. My mother is *pissed!*"

I wanted to protect them. I didn't want them to see me cower from my mother. Each blow I intervened inside my shell. The blows.

"Please! Please go home!" I pleaded, imagining the worst. "My mother stopped. I think I wore her out." I chuckled, hoping they believed me. I knew better. My mother was on the other side of the front door, waiting to kill her prey.

"It is okay. She probably has gone into her bedroom."

Again, I did not believe those words. Terror filled my veins.

I did not want them to witness my death.

"It is fine. She will leave me alone." I knew it was not over. I will never be over. *Never!*

I labeled this beating the *boxing match.*

I was the *loser!* Without a doubt, I would not win.

I walked back into the house. My face hit the tile again. The front door slammed *shut.* My mother punched my cheek with a closed fist. Mother hammered my eyes shut. Swollen shut... Blood flooded from my nose.

Nothing would silence the *boxer* (*Mother*). She wore leather gloves, which felt like steel weights. My head bled and was swollen too.

"Get going, you piece of shit!" Mother grabbed my shirt, and pinched my sides, and twisted her fingernails into my flesh. "Get going! Ride them, Cowboy!"

Mother's cowboy boots kicked my side, stirring and directing my every movement. Her kicks hit my head and my face. She was able to control my head by using my bloody, matted hair like a bridle. She pulled my hair harder if I did not move fast enough. Mother enjoyed the control over my pain. I buckled underneath her weight and power.

"*Oh yeah*, your friend's parents called me at work earlier. They demanded to know the truth as to why their precious children were late getting home from prom."

So this was why my mother was so pissed. Now I understand what set her off to beat me senseless.

"What did you tell them?" My heart sunk further into my stomach. I feared what my mother told them than the beating I received. "What did you tell them?" My thoughts were of *panic*. Mother wanted to have another round of boxing on my body. "Please tell me."

I whispered a silent prayer, "God, please help me!" My prayers were unanswered.

"Well, first, I spoke to Patrick's father..." My mother expression showed how proud she was and very proud of the conversation between parents. My mother had *no remorse, no regrets.*

Crystal Dawn White, high-school picture junior year 1981
1982 choir picture: *far left—middle row,* Crystal dawn white

Chapter Nineteen

ESCAPE PLAN

Ivy's face was ash colored. Beautiful olive skin tone, her black hair framed her daring black-coal eyes. She had a strong Hebrew nose along with Ivy's amazon build at five feet, seven inches. She showed not only beauty on the skin, but in her heart. Today Ivy's complexion was pale.

"Crystal, I begged my mom to get you out of here!" We both were sitting on Johnny's queen-size bed. It was part of the matching bedroom set, with two nightstands, a long dresser, and the three attached mirrors.

I looked at the mirror, watching Ivy. Her face had no smile, only tears. Her usual beaming smile showed her pearl-white teeth. Yet today there was no smile, no laughter. Ivy sat motionless, considering her words carefully while holding my hand.

"Your mother almost killed you! I know if Patrick and I did not show yesterday, I think your mother would have killed you!" Ivy's fingers traced the lines on my palm. "Both of us saw your mother's rage. Nothing would *stop* her! We yelled and threatened your mother. She kept beating you" Ivy's hand gripped my hand tighter. Ivy's tears fell on my shoulder.

I had no more tears. I felt no emotions. I could not even the feel cracked ribs or the swollen lips. My eyes burned from the salty tears from last night. I was cry uncontrollably. *Now!* There are no tears left to cry!

"Listen, Crystal! My mom is coming get you tomorrow, I promise. I explained to my mom how deadly close you were to being inside a coffin." Ivy seemed to be convincing herself as well as me. "I know my mom will help!" Under her breath, she said, "My mom has to *help!*"

I noticed that Ivy brought a large suitcase resting against her leg.

"Put what you need to take with you. Like important papers and special mementos. Do not worry about clothes. I will give you some of mine."

Ivy placed the suitcase on the bed.

She cupped my chin, and looking directly into my eyes, she said, "You are my sister not by blood, but by *hearts.*"

Ivy went into my bedroom, opening dresser drawers, searching for items that I might need.

"Crystal, please be careful. Especially tonight. Start getting things together. I will take the suitcase back to my house."

We searched through my closet, all the corners of my bedroom, not missing anything.

We closed the suitcase. Ivy gave me a huge hug and a kiss on the cheek.

"C'mon, your mother will be home in a couple of hours." Ivy went to the front door, and turning around, she said, "I will leave you a cute outfit to wear tomorrow. Your mother can not accuse you of stealing."

Ivy was right—the less I took of my own, the better.

"Crystal, I will not be able to see you before you leave. You know my phone number. I will be going to school and keeping myself busy. I need to act surprised when I am questioned about your disappearance."

Ivy talked in a gentle voice, "I am so sorry you will miss going to Disneyland for Senior Day. You are in my thoughts and prayers. *I love you!*" Ivy gave me one more hug as tears streamed down her face. Tears rolled down my face.

I needed to prepare myself for a big day *tomorrow!*

Ivy Lazarre, 1982
senior picture,
Walnut High School

1974 chestnut creek
Diamond Bar, California

First, I mowed and raked the front and backyard. I made sure the dogs were watered and fed. I felt terrible that I could not take both Trika and Shampoo with me.

Both dogs were Russian borzoi. My mother started participating in *dog* shows. She wanted to prance with the dogs and tried to fit in the circle of dog shows' social world. But now she grew tired of the dog shows; this meant that the two Russian borzoi would be tossed aside, like everything else Mother became bored with. Mother's new hobby was the Quarter Horse world.

I would plead and beg my mother to buy dog food. Instead, my mother instructed me to make pancakes and feed the dogs, who whimpered and howled because they were hungry. I would give them food from my plate or anything I was able to find to feed them. Late at night the silence would pierce from the howls. They were hungry.

I pushed my hand through my bedroom window. I was frustrated with not being able to feed or care for these two beautiful animals.

Johnny, mother's new lover, replaced the windowpane more than once. He also would buy the dog food.

Leaving was becoming harder and harder to accomplish. I cleaned the house. Started cleaning the rooms that would not be used tonight. I wanted to make sure all my chores were completed by 10:00 AM. My mother left for work at 9:30 AM.

Standing in the kitchen, watching the clock, it reminded me that my mother would be home shortly, which meant I better start preparing Mother's dinner.

She started a diet, "*Lose twenty pounds in two weeks.*" Therefore, I had to follow the directions to a T.

I had about an hour to spare. I changed the bed linen, made the beds. I cleaned and prepared for my escape tomorrow. I was counting down to the very last second.

Putting my mother's dinner on a plate, I had a flashback to last summer. My mother gained fifty pounds. She forced me to eat only pancakes breakfast, lunch, and dinner.

Mother said, "You better gain weight and weigh the same as I do!"

My mother was determined that I gained weight. She had me stand on the weight scale.

"You are only to eat pancakes for three weeks. Breakfast, lunch, and dinner. So you better gain weight and weigh the same as I *do!*"

My mother was determined that I gain the weight. She would place me on the scale. At this time, I weighed 105 pounds. I was just as determined not to gain any weight. Every time Mother had me stand on the scale, I lost weight. My mother watched my food intake.

I would run up and down a steep hill. It was three-block downward climb. I ran before and after school, from the school bus drop-off to my home. I had to take summer school because of my absences during the school year.

Mother made sure I ate the pancakes in front of her, every crumb of the pancake and butter dripping with syrup inhaled through my mouth.

The third week of eating only pancakes, I stood on the weight scale. I held my breath. I prayed I did not gain an ounce. I weighed less than when I began the pancake diet. I manage to lose five pounds. I *now* weighed one hundred pounds.

My pants and shirts hung loosely over my skeleton frame.

"What the *hell!*" Mother slapped the side of my head. "You lost weight, and I *gained* another ten pounds!" She shoved me off the weight scales; her rage made me smile inside. It was a blessing Mother didn't win this victory!

I had won this one!

I beamed and laughed inside my thoughts. I was humming a triumph song, a melody of happiness, "*I won. I won!*"

Mother's rage boiled over. Pushing with all her might, my face landed into the bathroom floor. Not even her bare feet kicked my stomach. She was powerless to bring tears of pain. Mother's big toe jammed into the bathroom rug. This made her angrier, which landed harder kicks into my hips, stomach, and my pelvic area.

"You are a *bitch!*" she screamed at the top of her voice, wailing more punches on my head and face.

Oh yeah, I won! I was not able to stop the abuse, but I could control my thoughts, my body, my heart, and soul! Each hit and kick was worth it...*I won!*

The headlights beamed through the dining-room sliding, door. Mother slammed the driver's car door shut. Moving at a fast pace to the front door, I already expected Mother was in a foul mood. Mother slammed the car door then the front door, which was a different telltale sign—it was going to be a *bad* night.

"*Damn*, Jack!" Mother hissed after slamming the front door behind her. "Jack is always making me look bad and stupid!" she said with another slam of her work papers on the dining-room table. Bang! Her purse fell to the tiled floor…I scrambled to pick her purse off the floor, spilling the contents.

Jack was one of the employees that worked with my mother at the House of Cutlery in the West Covina Mall, California. I also worked at the store on Saturdays and Sundays and holidays.

Once in a while I would work during the summers and special store sells.

The House of Cutlery was a Mom and *Pop* small business, selling all brands of knives from household cutlery to professional chef knives. My favorite knife were the Japanese samurai swords. The best-selling knife was the Swiss Army.

"BULLSHIT! Jack is full of *shit!*"

Mother had not noticed me picking up her purse, or that I spilled most of the contents next to her. Mother finally noticed me, and her attention did waver from her rant and raving.

"Jack told Bob [the owner of the store] that I am stealing inventory and money." Moher, catching her breath, continued yelling, "And that Jack should be responsible to check the inventory against the balance sheet. If the inventory did not match with the sale of the knives, I should be accountable for the price or product!" Mother was still yelling while she headed to her bedroom. "I have to go into work two hours early and find the errors, or be ready to find a new job."

I knew Jack spoke the truth about Mother and the inventory. I have watched Mother put knives and certain items in her large purse at least half a dozen times.

Sometimes Mother came home after her shift at work and empty her purse, revealing the stolen cutlery. Most of the stolen product was in the hall closet, waiting for someone's birthday, wedding, or anniversary. Mother had the perfect gift wrapped.

"*Crissy!* Bring me a glass of red wine with my dinner."

I hated when my mother called me *Crissy*. It was Mother's way of telling me there would be a beating tonight. Mother's nickname for me sealed my fate for the remaining of the evening. Mother was filled with *hate* and *anger*!

It was going to be *hell night!*

I poured the wine in a large stem glass. Then I arranged Mother's dinner perfectly on her plate, exactly how she liked.

Mother sat straight in her bed. I placed the dinner tray on her lap. She fumbled through channels on TV and finally located one of her favorite game-show programs.

"Don't think I haven't noticed how chummy you and Jack are."

The statement was true, Jack and I did have chats. Nothing more than a friendship.

"You and him, always joking behind my back. I bet you did not think I watch you both?" This was more of a statement, not really a question. "You flirt with your tiny butt and your sly smile." Mother pushed her dinner plate away from her, and with a full mouth of food, she continued with more insults regarding my body, "You push your tits into Jack's face, batting your eyes!"

Mother squeezed a hard-boiled egg between her fingers. Then she crammed the egg into her mouth. Pieces of the egg fell on mother's nightgown. With no warning, Mother gagged on the hard-boiled egg. She coughed it up in her hand. With little effort, Mother threw the discarded egg at me. Moving slightly, the egg hit the bedroom doorframe. Leaning over to pick up the small pieces left of the egg, my nightgown ripped along thinning stitches at the back.

"What an *ass* you are. Your nothing butt an *ass!* Your *ass* is getting too *big!* Take off that night gown!" Mother watched my every movement. I took off the flannel nightgown. I always wore a T-shirt over my night clothes. I lifted off my T-shirt and nightgown, trying to keep my breasts covered with my empty arms. I was wearing a holey granny underwear. I tied a knot in the elastic to hold up the underwear from falling around my ankles.

"*Oh* my god! Your breasts are uneven." Mother chuckled and clapped her hands together. "You are deformed as well as stupid. What man is going to want to be with a retarded and deformed, ugly woman?" Mother sipped her wine, her twisted smile being amuse of my physically deformed body. I was still holding my arms securely over my bare breasts.

"What a retard I have given birth to. Your right-side breast is higher than your left. You better pray you marry soon and keep your deformed breasts a secret. God, you make me want to vomit!" Waving her hand, she said, "Get dressed." She changed her mind. "Turn your *ass* around. I am curious to see what Jack seems to admire about your *ass!* I like to admire such disgusting creature I gave birth to!" Turning slowly, Mother inspected my butt.

"Get dressed, you worthless piece of *shit!*"

Mother took delight in herself, finding flaws with my body. This became the best part of Mother's evening—Mother's disgusting, unwanted child, who *no one loved!*

"Tsk, tsk! What a shame. Poor little Crissy, deformed like a retard!"

Mother repeated this verse over and over like a nursery rhyme.

Rhyming words to my sadness. "You are a disgusting piece of shit!"

My face became hot with embarrassment. I am a *retard! Deformed, born in hell!* This is all I am and *good* for!

"Hey, lazy *ass*, clean up that egg!" Mother pointed to the squashed boiled egg stuck on the carpet and bedroom doorjamb. I started to pick the egg off the white shag carpet. "*No, eat it!* Waste not. *Not* want!"

I started removing the fine black Doberman dog fur off the demolished boiled egg. "NO! NO! Eat it that way. I don't care that there is dog hair in it. *Lazy bitches* and *lazy retards* should eat this way!"

Stuffing the egg and dog hair in my mouth, my throat tightened. I held the vomit inside my throat. I was trying very hard not to choke or cough. I somehow I managed neither to cough nor throw up.

"You better not throw up. I will make you eat it off the floor too!"

Swallowing hard, I was thinking about other things. I kept both egg and fur down. I just repeated to myself, "Swallow, get it down," reciting the words over and over.

"Come here, little Crissy," she said, waving her empty wine glass at me. "You need to refill my glass." This was her second glass. Hopefully, Mother would become tipsy and fall asleep soon.

"Here, my *lazy piggy*. Drink the rest of the wine that is in the bottle. You better drink it all. No drop left in it. Drink 'til it is all gone." Mother held the bottle to my lips, and I felt the wine spilling into my throat. "Bottoms *up!*" She added, "You *retard.*"

I felt I was drowning, trying to swallow as fast as Mother poured the wine down my throat. Staggering backward, Mother let the wine bottle fall to the white carpet. A tiny amount of wine trickled onto the carpet.

Mother swung her legs off the bed, kicking her foot at my head. My face felt the worse of the assault. Another kick, a fist on the back of my head, pushed my face into the spilled red wine staining carpet.

"Waste *not!* Want *not!*" Mother pushed my head harder until I smelled the odor of the spilled wine. "Like a little retarded piggy." My lips tasted the wine.

"Get a towel, and you better get the stain out of my beautiful white carpet." Mother released my head, walked to the bathroom, and tossed a towel at the mess on the floor.

"*Oh* Crissy, Crissy!" Singing and skipping, my mother recited my name on her way to the kitchen.

I finished cleaning the red-wine stain from the white carpet. A wet spot remained. Throwing the bath towel in the hamper and the empty wine bottle in the trash can, I sighed, believing the temper rage of Mother's was over. *Wrong!* I was never so *wrong!*

"*Crissy, Crissy,* stand right here in the doorway! Stay right there all night. *All night!* A lazy *bitch* does not deserve to sit or lay on furniture."

Mother sang and hummed as she poured another glass of wine. Missing her wine glass and pouring the wine on the night stand, she held the empty glass to me.

"Pour me my wine, Miss Retard."

She demanded me to hurry and not spill one ounce of the precious wine either. She tormented and insulted me while she moved her glass back and forth, daring me to miss her glass. Her laughed of hate, snaring from her grinding teeth. Somehow, I did manage to keep pace with her movements.

"Don't miss! If you know what is *good* for *you*!" She was hitting my arm, trying to make me spill the wine.

Soon she was bored with the mouse-and-cat game.

Once again, I won this match!

"I am tired. Get over to the door and place your nose in the crack of the door. Better not move either, little piggy!" I started to put the half-full bottle of wine on the nightstand.

"*No.* You hold the wine bottle."

Snarling, she threw her pillow at my back. Staggering from the impact of the heavy goose pillow, I stood with my back toward Mother. I held a death grip on the bottle.

I felt tipsy from drinking the wine earlier. Standing upright and straight, I did not allow my mother to find another reason or fault with me this night. Finally, Mother started to snore, a wonderful sound! I needed to pee so bad! I tried to be quiet. I tiptoed to the bathroom closer to the kitchen.

Leaning on the hallway walls for support and keeping my balance, I was *not making a sound!*

I did it!

Mother didn't wake up! Thank you, *God!*

Pulling myself toward the bathroom sink, I was holding onto it for dear life. I was able to sit on the toilet. I was praying not to make a sound, not to wake my mother. Looking down at my left hand, I had the wine bottle glued between my fingers. My head was woozy, so light. I stood up; my head was so heavy. I was swaying back and forth, as if I was on the ocean. From side to side, I flushed the toilet.

I stood silently, listening for my mother's voice. Drawing my breath with shallow inhales, I heard my mother's snoring.

Great!

I was carrying the wine bottle as I headed to the kitchen. "*Why does my head weigh so heavy? and I am dizzy.*" Questioning myself, I found *no answer*. I was searching for something, but, *what?* Not sure why I even went to the kitchen. I opened drawers, and the last drawer was the knife drawer. Not here. I searched the knife block. This was exactly what I wanted. Choosing the biggest, and sharpest, and longest blade, *hell yeah! The butcher knife!*

Staring at the huge, cool blade resting against my arm, I leaned into the kitchen sink, pulling my arm inside the basin. I slowly hacked the butcher blade on my wrist, arm, and fingers.

One cut, two cuts, and another *cut.* No longer keeping count of each slash from the butcher knife, I was cutting my flesh as if melted butter.

No pain!

No sadness!

I feel nothing! Nothing!

"*Wait!*" I told myself.

My brain was coming *alive!*

"Mother should see this. It isn't fair, not letting Mother watch. Witness her retarded daughter killing herself?" Am I not her little "*Crissy!*" Covering my bloody arm with a dish towel, holding onto the wine bottle again, I cradled the bottle in the curve of my uninjured arm.

My victory, my trophy, the wine bottle.

Damn, the dish towel was soaked through with my deep-red blood. Soon all this will finally, *end! No more* words slashing my *heart! No more* tormenting cursing insults! I smiled to myself...

I walked toward my mother while she slept, unaware of the horror I was about to reveal. Putting my trophy (wine bottle) on her nightstand, I removed the soak dish towel. I stabbed my wrist, another cut along the vein. The victory was my victory, my *death!*

Slash-cut number *four!*

Slash-cut number *five*. Number five, deep, slashed cuts. My skin flapped open, gashes of blood tracing form my arm onto the white carpet. The blood was no longer a drip; it was rushing as a river down my fingertips. My eyelids began to grow weary and tired. It was almost impossible to keep my eyes open. I was tired. I focused on my mother sleeping soundly. Not able to hold the knife, it fell to the carpet. The dish towel also slid off my damaged arm onto mother's bed. Soaked bloody dish towel laid over the edge of mother's side of the bed, dripping, leaving a pool of my broken soul on the wake of my *death!* The color red spread onto the bed sheets as a claw creeping toward Mother's sleeping body. With little effort, the dish towel slipped to the floor. My head dazed, I watched the imprints from both the knife and towel. The impression left not only my blood, but my wounded soul, laying at Mother's feet.

A black film clouded my eyes. My mind engulfed into darkness. My knees buckled, catching to hold the side of mattress, steadying my balance. Retrieving the bloody dish towel, "Don't make a mess," my mind instructed my fingers and arm. Wrapping the injured arm once again with the soaked dish towel, not able to see clearly, I was feeling the material on the bedsheets, tangled into the mangled arm that dangled, showing muscle to bone.

"What the *hell!*" Mother's alarm clock sounded with the time at 6:00 AM.

"Am I dreaming? Did I imagine cutting myself?" I questioned myself. "It was so vivid! So *real!*"

"Get up! You *lazy* piece of *shit!*" Mother shoved and pushed my body.

"Get my coffee!" Mother stepped over me. She did not notice the blood-stained carpet or the bloody handprints on the bedsheets. Mother walked to the bathroom. I pulled the blanket and pillows over the bloody mess.

"GET UP!" Am I hearing things? Did I really hear someone speak?

I felt pressure being applied on the wounds of my arm.

Mikheal, my *wonderful* guardian angel, knelt by my side.

"I told you, I shall never leave *you!*" Mickheal's angelic voice was so melliferous. "I always stayed with you. You are my beautiful girl. I promised to keep you safe." Mickheal's eyes burned into my sunken body.

"I kept my promise. I shall never leave you. *Never!*" Mickheal escorted me through the bathroom near the kitchen.

Removing the soiled dish towel, I allowed the warm water from the facet pour over my arm into the cuts.

Carefully washing the fresh and dried blood from my wounds, even after the slashed flesh healed, the scars were a reminder of my wounded soul, *not* wanting to live anymore. The scars were my victory to a *future* I deserved.

"*God*, your *Heavenly Father*, never left you. The *Lord Jesus Christ* knows and feels your *pain*. Your torment to stop your heartbeats. Taking your precious life, that is not the answer either. *God* is not able to change the choices your mother made. You belong in *God's* hands. You are his *child*. Lord Jesus Christ knows your heart. He sends guardian angels as soldiers, bringing a shield and swords to protect his wonderful children. I tried to stop you, *Crystal!* I screamed into your thoughts. It is you not wanting to *hear!*"

Mickheal's face clouded with sadness.

Oh, Mickheal, my dearest angel. My guardian angel. You could not intervene against human actions. My deepest darkness I prayed for. Thank goodness I was not successful. *I wanted to live...* I choose to live... *God*, he has a purpose for me. Mickheal wiped and soothed my tears and fears. I had a reminder how much I had to live for. God had a purpose for me.

"You are worthy. You are *God's* child. I will never give up on you, and *God* will never give up on you! I will *never* leave you, *never!*" Mikheal held me close, and for a brief moment, I felt safe.

Mother's voice broke the silence. Goosebumps crawled up my skin.

"Crystal, where's my breakfast and coffee?"

Mikheal left my side. His melody harp voice lingering, "*God* has a purpose for you. You are *God's* child!"

Going to the kitchen, I poured Mother's coffee. I placed her breakfast on flowered plate: two boiled eggs, two slices dry toast, half a grapefruit, and a whole cup of plain yogurt. I carried Mother's breakfast to her at the dining-room table. Glazing at clock above Mother's head, it was 7:30 AM.

Mrs. Lazzarre (Ivy's mother) would be picking me up soon. I had two and half hours to get ready. *My escape!*

Mother was in her bathroom, looking at her image in the mirror.

I wanted to say, "Mirror, mirror on the wall, who is the worst mother of them *all.*" I already knew the reply. "Your mean, ugly, and black-hearted, cruel mother is the worst of them all by far!" the mirror would say.

"Bring me more coffee, you lazy bitch!" Mother glared at me through her mirror.

"Great morning. Mother already started with the insults. This is why I needed to leave." My answer from Mother's lips.

"Hurry up, you lazy cow," she said as I brought her coffee. "Brush my hair. I want it put in a French twist. *Hurry up!* I am running late."

Seeing my reflection in Mother's mirror, standing behind her, I carefully placed and secured bobby pins into her hair. I noticed when I raised my arm, blood and open cuts could be seen. Pulling my nightgown sleeve to cover the wounds, I changed my clothes. Put another clean dish towel over the injured arm. I didn't want Mother to ask about the towel, or what I'm hiding. I took Mother's empty breakfast plate in the kitchen sink.

Finishing Mother's hair, I started to apply mother's makeup. I was *daydreaming*. Soon I would escape this nightmare. This *hell!*

"Time to be patient," I whispered to myself. "Remember, this will be the last time you will ever have to be mother's *slave. Never, never again!*

My stomach was doing belly flips; butterflies flew around inside my tummy.

"Soon, you will be safe!"

"Damn it! A lazy bitch you are. One of my eyelids has more blue eye shadow than the other eyelid." Mother's attention spied a stain

on her blue blouse laying on her bed. "Get me another blouse out my closet. And fix my eye shadow. It still doesn't look right." I tried making both eyelids look evenly. I ironed the blouse I chose.

Mother had not noticed the dried blood on my arm or the carpet. I was keeping the blanket on the top bloody mess.

8:30 AM. One hour and thirty minutes left. I will leave, never to worry again. I will leave the bloody mess on Mother's side bed and carpet. Let her clean IT!

My life would *begin!* My adventure would *start!* My dreams would come *true.*

"Get my lunch. Start the car. Better not spill any of my coffee, like you did yesterday!"

I did spill Mother's coffee yesterday. Mother pinched my skin under my arm and twisted the skin with her fingernails. I jerked from her abuse. The coffee spilled.

Finally! Mother left for work.

I will be leaving soon!

9:00 AM. Oh my *gosh!* I need to get my things together.

Take a shower. Last shower in this dungeon. Dressing myself in baggy pants and shirt, this would be the last time I will wear torn and faded, which showed my toes through the fabric and rubber soles.

I was heading toward *freedom!* I opened the front door with one last glance at my prison.

"Goodbye!"

Never! Never will I walk through these doors again!

10:00 a.m. Freedom!

Chapter Twenty

NO MORE TEARS, NO MORE PAIN

Mrs. Lazarre parked next to the side curb, hiding behind the blooming yellow hedge. Oncoming traffic unaware, Mrs. Lazarre was my savior, releasing me from a bolted prison gates, my *hell!* Guarding and being my warden for seventeen years of my childhood life.

10:00 AM. I carried my backpack, with my personnel papers, Social Security Card, birth certificate, and school report cards. Amazing how my seventeen years fit inside into a small satchel.

Taking one last look at the prison's invisible cell bars, I would not be chained to my *past*. I was free to go into the *present*. My future belonged to *me!* Locking the front door with the dead bolt, I would never be jailed between these walls *again!*

I ran to Mrs. Lazarre's waiting getaway car. I escaped! My sadness, the evilness, and the hopelessness I once felt, forever left behind. Jumping into the back seat, I slid to the floor of the passenger side, keeping myself lowered from view, not wanting anyone to see me or notice the vehicle I escape in.

"Mrs. Lazarre, can we stop by the post office? I am expecting congratulation cards and information from Walnut High School." I was hoping my step-grandmother Smith also sent me a card and a few dollars.

"Sure, stay down. I'll tell you the coast is clear." Mrs. Lazarre was a careful driver and extremely cautious at this time.

"Okay, coast is clear."

Mrs. Lazzarre drove to entrance of the post-office doors. Walking through the double glass door, the mailbox straight ahead, I searched through mail, mostly addressed to *Mrs. White.* Yes, I had three graduation cards: one from my step-grandmother, another from Johnny Miller, the last one Bob (owner of House of Cutlery). Placing the other mail in the mailbox, I gazed at the other glass door opposite of the ones I entered. I stopped in my tracks. *Oh shit!* My mother drove up to the post office. I knew that black-and-orange-colored car anywhere.

Making my way to the glass doors I entered, I paced my steps with mother's steps. As she entered, I exited. The sunlight covered my actions. Thank you, *God…* The reflecting sun blocked my escape.

Mrs. Lazarre watched the scene play out in front of her. She opened the passenger door. I crawled and slipped onto the back seat, slimming onto floorboard.

Mother waved and mumbled, "*Hello,*" to Mrs. Lazarre. With a slight wave back to mother, Mrs. Lazarre smiled.

"Stay down!" Mrs. Lazarre spoke under her breath with a smile and slight wave. Mrs. Lazarre, kept her eyes on my mother's every movement.

"*Oh,* thank goodness, your mother is too busy looking through her mail." Mrs. Lazarre's hands trembled as she steered out of the post-office parking lot.

"Let's get you to my house and get everything you need together." It took ten minutes driving on the freeway to get to Mrs. Lazarre's home. But it seemed like hours!

With a push of her garage-door remote, the door lifted upward, giving permission for the fugitive to enter the sanctuary.

She pulled her car forward all the way, fitting closely among the boxes and assorted keepsakes. Tight squeeze…

Mrs. Lazarre sighed a large, deep breath of relief.

Looking down at the tossed cards, I kept a death grip on my backpack.

"It's safe. Climb on out!" Mrs. Lazarre whispered as the garage door closed. Mrs. Lazarre praised God for delivering her and her package home safe.

Yes, it was a narrow escape. My heart jumped with the excitement of *freedom!*

Mrs. Lazarre placed her hands on my quivering shoulders.

"Crystal, before Lorrie picks you up, I need to explain really important things to you," she spoke while ushering me the dining-room table. Pulling out a chair, she gestured to sit.

"It is extremely important that you listen to every word and instruction I tell you to do," she said, pouring a soft drink into a large glass filled with ice cubes. Mrs. Lazarre handed the drink to me and also sat down next to me. Putting her hand over mine, drumming her fingers entwined with shaking hands, she spoke calmly and slowly, "Crystal, what I am doing, in helping you leave home, could and would place me in *jail.* You and I both know without question or doubts, your mother would have me prosecuted. Probably a very lengthy sentence too. If your mother ever became aware that it was me, my family and I, who assisted you in any way, your mother would not *stop* until I am locked up and the key thrown away!"

Searching Mrs. Lazarre's face, seeing the fear that I could cause Ivy's entire family, I stated, "*Why?* You saved *me!*"

Mrs. Lazzarre again tapped her fingers in mine and answered, "*Yes!* But the law and your mother might see things differently. Do you *understand?*"

Pulling my chin up and looking into my eyes, she waited for my reply.

"*Yes*, I understand. It is *not* fair!" I mumbled. Yet I agreed.

"Yes, you are right, it is not fair. I want you to promise me you will not write Ivy. Ivy cannot know any details of where or how and who assisted you in leaving home."

I nodded.

"Ivy must not lie. The only way to do this, you may not contact her." Again, I nodded, *yes*.

"Never tell anyone that it is *me* who got you out of that hell!" Mrs. Lazarre stood up and looked out her front window.

"Time for you to change and make sure you put all the cases you are taking by the kitchen back door."

Walking into Ivy's bedroom, there, on her bed, was a cute sundress and sandals next to the dress. Laying on top of the clothes, Ivy left a sweet handwritten note: *Please stay safe! I love you, sister of hearts.*

Putting the clothes on, I felt a change inside of mind. I felt true *happiness.* Placing the clothes I wore earlier inside my suitcase, I made sure there were no traces of me being at Ivy's home.

"I know you must be very scared. Look at this as an adventure. A brand-*new beginning!* How exciting to start a life that is going to be filled with so much *joy,* and you make your own *happy ending!*"

Mrs. Lazarre gave me encouraging words, just as Lorrie drove onto the driveway.

Baby-blue Pinto was my chariot to my next map to *freedom!*

"I better open the garage." Mrs. Lazarre waved Lorrie through the garage door. Lorrie's car bumper was scraping paint with Mrs. Lazarre's car.

"Hello, little Crissy!" Lorrie said, with her bubbling laughter and innocent of pure, careful *soul!*

"Here are Crystal's suitcases and backpack." Mrs. Lazarre placed my bags into the Pinto's hatch back trunk.

"You better get going. It will be lunch soon. Los Angeles traffic is bumper-to-bumper."

Mrs. Lazarre hugged and kissed me over and over. Grabbing my palm, she cuffed a hundred dollars into my hand and closed it into a fist.

"Remember what I said, no one is to know that either I or Ivy helped you. You know that I could lose my freedom and family. Please keep our secret until I die."

Clapping a tissue to her nose, she wiped her nose periodically, saying, "At least until I am six feet under, then it would not matter." Mrs. Lazarre dabbed tissue to her teared eyes. Mrs. Lazzarre gave Lorrie a tight hug, and she spoke with a stern voice.

"Be careful, extra careful, on the freeway." Lorrie and I got into Lorrie's car. She waved and said, "*Goodbye.*"

I did not see or speak to Mrs. Lazarre again. I missed her smiles, her laughter, and most of all, her motherly kindness, which has lasted forever in my heart to this day. The memories and joy I enjoyed in my life after my parent's home were of endless thank yous to Mrs. Lazzarre. Her voice sweetly saying "*goodbye*" was really my "*hello*" to a new beginning.

I crouched down on Lorrie's car floor, out of sight.

"Crissy, you will be *fine!* Stay down a while longer. I will let you know when we get on the freeway." Lorrie didn't have to inform me the freeway was approaching. She was a free spirit. She also drove like a free spirit too.

Lorrie drove like the *devil* was after her. She drove very fast!

Lorrie slammed on her touchy brakes. All else fell; as the traffic light turned yellow, she drove faster. Lorrie burned rubber from her car tires, screeching as she gunned the car engine. Lorrie also believed no traffic coming from other directions during a red light, Lorrie would drive through red lights and stop signs. At this time of years, there were no such things as cameras at traffic signals. I am pretty sure Lorrie would be able to talk herself out of a ticket from a traffic cop. Green lights, drive fast; yellow lights, drive faster; red lights, questionable. No traffic—go even faster. With Lorrie's ability to go around corners, you better hold on tight and enjoy the fish tale of drifting.

Lorrie could use the emergency brake gracefully.

I hit the side of Lorrie's car doors more times than I could count. I met her gear shift on a few occasions. *I am free!*

Thank goodness! I thought as Lorrie drove onto the 405 freeway. With the car windows down, wind blowing in my face, I felt *freedom.* I could smell the ocean, it smelled of *freedom!*

"Okay, little Crissy. We are on the 405 freeway. You can breathe and have peace."

Lorrie's laugh and her expression reminded me of Minnie Mouse, the cartoon character. Her voice was the sweetest sound and adorable sister of *hearts.*

Lorrie personality, is like Betty Boop!

I loved this wonderful, beautiful free spirit.

"I bet you are so *happy* to get out of the *hellhole!*"

Lorrie pushed different radio-station buttons, trying to locate her favorite music station. With a clear channel, the song, *We Only Just Begun,* one of The Carpenters' great songs blared through the speakers.

Perfect song to be playing on the radio. I kept this song close to my heart, my escape song, my thoughts said.

"Lorrie, when did Mrs. Lazarre get ahold of you?"

Lorrie, still fiddling with the music-tuning dial, replied, "Ivy called me last night. I could not understand Ivy very well. Ivy was crying and in hysterics. Ivy handed the phone to her mother."

Lorrie looked at me with concern. "The plan was completed with three people who truly love you. This plan is perfect. No one will even think it is me who picked you up since I haven't been around for several months." Lorrie directed her attention to the slowing traffic in front of her. Out exit off the freeway was Bellflower off-ramp.

"You're going to love being mine and Scott's roommate. I am so excited. We will have a great time." Lorrie's expression changed into a sober-sad stare at my bandaged arm.

"Did your mother do that?"

"No, I did this myself. Last night. I wanted the pain to stop. I felt so much anger and *hate* towards my mother. I could not take her cruel words, her beatings, and this ugliness that I am failing to everyone." Rubbing the hidden cuts on my arm, I could feel the sensation of each deep cut lashed into my flesh.

"Another hour, *we* will be at your new home!" Lorrie focused on the slow snail pace of cars entering and leaving the off-ramps off the freeway.

"Where we live, it's an hour from the Long Beach Ocean. I can hardly wait to start getting a suntan."

Lorrie already looked amazing. Every detail of her body—the typical southern Valley girl. Lorrie was a perfect image of wholesome.

Remembering the last time I stepped on the beach, it was during a UCLA cattle call (interview with directors etc.). UCLA students studied correct technics: use of lightening, film, camera, props, and location for movie site. I wanted the experience and résumé for a movie credentials. (I should say my mother wanted it.) The following weekend, after interview, Mother and I headed to Santa Barbra's sandy beaches. A wonderful misty fog rolled over the crew and actors. I had a few freckles, waist-long strawberry blond, and enjoyed the other two boys, who also played jokingly into the ocean waves. I was able to stay under the radar until the makeup and wardrobe lady questioned the scars on my arms and legs.

"I fell on my bike," was my reply.

Filming ended, and Mother acted like dutiful mother.

I turned into a sunburned lobster wearing a two-piece bathing suit. The top and bottoms had a gold emblem, with left hearts on each side of the white bottoms, and one heart between the breast from the top. On the bottom of the bikini, each side had a heart-shaped cutout. The heart shape showed when I got sunburned.

"You are going to *love* it! All of it!" Lorrie said as she merged into the off-ramp headed to Bellflower.

I looked at the cars and the houses lining the streets.

"Lorrie, how long have you and Scott been living together?

"About a month. I met Scott at the Sunshine Club in LA."

Lorrie seemed to be reading my thoughts.

"I had a fake ID. Plus, Scott knows the owner, his name is Rudy. The male dancers are so *hot!*" Listening to Lorrie talking about her life, the excitement of her life, I am envious.

"Scott and I hit it off, like, right away. I cannot say we are deeply in *love*. We do *love* each other's company." Lorrie giggled.

"What kind of work does Scott do?"

"Scott has his own business. He is a plumber." Lorrie turned down the car down a dead-end street.

Scott's and Lorrie's house was the only green one level. Attached garage peered from behind the rock driveway.

Looking at Lorrie, she was born to a wonderful mother and father. Both of her parents were well-known artists. Her father was a sculptor. Her mother, a watercolor artist. Lorries parents were divorced, yet remained close, raising Lorrie with a free spirit. Lorrie, was raised with *love* and *endless joy*. Lorrie's personality never changed though turmoil from either mankind or environmentalists.

I met Lorrie when she went to stay at her uncle's home. He lived across the street form Ivy's parents.

This was how Ivy, Lorrie, and I became bosom buddies. *Sisters of the heart.*

Lorrie was the most popular new girl attending Walnut High School.

She fell madly in love with Richard, a football player on varsity. The typical-jock attitude—conquer and damage the girl's reputation. Richard pretended to be a devoted boyfriend. A month after Lorrie and Richard dated, Lorrie was informed Richard was breaking off their relationship. He became a real *jerk*.

Lorrie would not *put out* (not have *sex*). Lorie commented, "Richard, did not want his pals to think that Richard lost his touch. And spread a rumor that I had sex with him."

196

Richard stopped calling Lorrie. Lorrie, a cheerleader, had no choice but to see Richard flirting with other girls.

He explained, "Can't be seen with you. You're not from the class of girls I go out with."

Richard broke Lorri's heart.

Lorrie tried to change almost everything about herself to be with Richard. Richard did not deserve Lorrie. Lorrie was on a higher platform than Richard would ever be on.

Lorrie moved back to her mother's home in Long Beach, California.

Lorrie could no longer face the insults, jeers from other cheer-leaders, and the comments from other *jocks*.

The students in Richard circle of friends would jeer and remark about Lorrie. Believing that Richard had another notch on belt, *jocks* and *cheerleaders* made it impossible for Lorrie to participate in the football rallies or on game day. Lorrie's heart shattered her lack of self-esteem all because of the cruel taunting from fellow students. Peer pressure controlled her past, not her *present* or *future!* Lorrie felt the only way to get a fresh start and leave the negativity was the decision to *move away!*

"We are here!" Lorrie drove down a short gravel driveway.

There was a small camper, which became my bedroom. The camper stood on silver stilts. It hovered over the manicured green grass. Little further down the pebble driveway was a studio apart-ment, very cuter cottage.

The entire property was a lined fenced yard. Every color rose bushes planted, giving a vibrate silky petals of a fairy tale. The front lawn was freshly cut, manicured with love.

"You will be staying in the camper. The house has only one bed-room and bathroom. Scott felt you needed privacy. The bathroom is the first door to your right when you enter from the back door."

Pulling my suitcase from the hatch back trunk, Lorrie opened the camper door. It was clean. A lot of room. I had a dining-room table, sink, and my bed above, enough room for one person. It was a darling setup.

It really was very cute. There was only room for one person to climb into the camper.

Perfect!

"I will give you private time to unpack, settle in. Scott will be home in about an hour." Lorrie closed the camper door, leaving me alone to gather my thoughts, to replay today's events.

"Am I really *free?*" I sat down at the little dining-room table.

I felt tired. I climbed up on the top and laid down on the bed.

Closing my eyes, I went into a deep slumber.

Freedom! Freedom! Freedom!

Two weeks had passed since my escape. I started feeling guilty about worrying my parents.

Did Mother worry about *me?*

Does she care if I am *alive* or *dead?*

I decided I would call my parent's house phone. I could leave a message on the answering machine. Let them know I am safe.

Mother would be at work.

I will just leave a message.

The house phone rang, and on the third ring, Johnny picked up the receiver.

"*Hello,*" Johnny's voice sounded hoarse and scratchy.

"Hello, Johnny. It's Crystal," I mumbled into the phone.

"Crystal? Crystal, do you know what you have done?" Johnny's voice was angry and demanding.

"I left home! I had to leave!" My hands were shaking, keeping the receiver from falling through my fingers.

"Steve is in *jail.*" Johnny's voice boomed into the phone. The echoing of his voice was in my ear.

"*Why?* What are you talking about? *Jail* for what?"

I sat down on the floor. The cord from the phone almost hanging me.

"Your mother found a ransom note. The one you put one front porch. She accused Steve of kidnapping and murdering you. Get ransom money. That is what your mother told the FBI agent. And that Steve was behind your disappearance."

I *never* imagined leaving home would could cause this terrible *mess!*

Kidnapping!
Murder!
What the hell!
Am I in *hell?*

"Johnny, I am fine! What can I do?"

Johnny seemed to calm down. But his voice was harsh.

"You need to call the Baldwin Police. I will give you the number with the detective's name. CALL HIM! Immediately after we hang up!" Johnny put the phone down to get the information. He returned to the phone.

"The detective's name is *John Young* The phone number 338-8431, file number #482-15000-1485-444. *Case Date* June 05, 1982. Call them immediately! Get Steve out of *jail!*" Johnny hung up the phone.

I was still on the floor, staring at the number and the detective's name.

My entire world has *ended*, crashing around me in a million pieces. Shaking, I dialed the phone number.

What do I tell the *police?* I questioned myself.

"Do I tell the police where I live?"

"Guess I won't know until I call them."

"May I speak to Detective John Young?" I spoke in a soft tone.

"Hello. Baldwin Police Department. How may I assist you?" the lady from dispatch asked.

"*Yes.* May I speak with Detective John Young?" I said, speaking a little louder. "I need to speak with him as soon as possible please." I built up more confidence as I spoke to the dispatcher.

"What is this regarding?' She asked.

Oh shit! What if they are tapping this call? I better talk fast and leave a message with her.

"Detective Young has left for the day. You may leave a message with me. I will make sure he receives the message when he comes in tomorrow."

"No, I will call back tomorrow. What time will he be in?" I did not want to leave Lorrie's phone number.

Lorrie walked into the house as I hung up the phone.

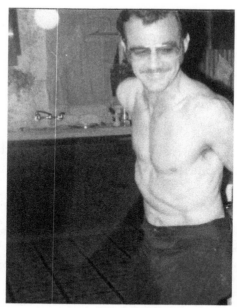

Johnny Miller (father to Steve Miller) 1978–1982

Richard A. White Sr.; Shirley Ann White (Kit),
Diamond Bar, California, January 1982
Last picture taken during me still living at home. Johnny
bought me the camera for Christmas (1981). Mother was
forty-for years of age. Father was fifty years of age.

House of Cutlery
170 Fashion Plaza
West Covina, CA 91790
 To that beautiful daughter of mine,
 She left home leaving no note behind.
 My daughter has broken my heart in two.
 Oh God, help me now, for I know not what to do.
 How much I love you, you'll never know.
 Oh, how you broke my heart and tore it away from my sole.
 I'm sorry for anything that I might have said or done.
 Please, please come and talk with me before the next setting of the sun.
 What more can I do? What more can I say?
 Except that we love you and pray that you are okay!
 Crystal, if you are okay and able to contact us, please call me at
 Home or at work. We love you!

       Your mother and father

August 23, 1982
Dearest Dennis,
 Hi! How are you? I am doing fine. I hope you are enjoying this beautiful weather.
 I am sorry we both missed my graduation. I am even more sorry I missed your Chili Pageant.
 Some things just cannot be helped.
 I left home in hope to find a future and happiness. I am not a very beautiful girl, nor even pretty. I should never have been in beauty pageants. Let alone the film industry. The atmosphere is for social, beautiful, and smart people.

I decided to join the service (Navy). I would like to be a successful attorney or writer.

I thought I should write you and explain the reasons for my leaving home. I also wanted to say thank you. I am very thankful that you have supported my mother, with advice, money, etc.

Please do not be disappointed with me. I think of you as part of my family.

I will write you again and let you know where I am stationed.

When you receive this letter, I will be eighteen.

I will be an adult. I am proud that I survived my youth.

I will speak to my mother when I am ready to talk with her.

At this time, it is not a smart idea to talk to her.

The issue is between my mother and myself. I hope you both will understand. I do think very highly of you. I can hope you feel the same for me.

I have caused more problems and trouble than I could ever imagine.

Take care. I hope we shall see and talk again.

At this time, I do not want anyone to know my whereabouts.

I am not a drug addict. I am not pregnant.

I want to stand on my own feet.

I am very capable of molding my future.

My decisions are mine. The path I walk is mine. Right or wrong.

I do hope I brought you peace and understanding.

Yours Truly,
Crystal D. White

Modeling, Catalina
Island, California, 1978

Modeling, Knottsberry Farm, California, 1978

Modeling at Disneyland, 1976

Picture taken by Dennis Chuchian

Chapter Twenty-One

ENDLESS WAKES / JUST A PUPPET

Endless Wakes

My dreams are the wisdom, but also ray failures.
I cannot go on, my mind is blank, my feelings are gone.
Now there is no more, no more tears, no more bad dreams.
The feelings have left my soul, days feel no endless, and
Nights remain so lonely.

Just a Puppet

I am just a puppet, plain old puppet.
I am just a puppet, plain old puppet.
Pull a string, watch me walk.
Pull another string, listen to me talk.
I want to be anything, anyone, but a puppet on a string.
I pretend I am *real*, a *real* heart, a *real* soul, a *real* person.
I want to be alive, breathe, be *me…anyone* but me, *anyone* but *me…*
I would pretend I am your queen.
You are my *forever* king.
I would pretend you were my *best*
Friend, we would always be together as one.
Pull a string, watch me walk.
Pull another string, listen to me talk.
I would pretend to be a ballerina dancer.
You were my tin soldier marching to conquer my heart.
I would pretend I could sing, while you played the drums,
Each beat, matching our heart beats as one.
Pull a string, watch me talk.
Pull another string, listen to me talk.
I would pretend I am a clown, making people laugh or cry with joy.
I want to be *real*, not just a puppet on a string.
Pull a string, watch me walk.
Pull another string, listen to me talk.
I would pretend I am the moon,
Lightening the sky through the nights,
I would pretend you are the sun,

Bringing each day a new sunrise.
Do we all have to pretend?
Trying to be someone we are not?
I am just a puppet, tossed on a dusty shelve.
Left alone with only memories to comfort me in the darkness.
Just a puppet, a plain old puppet. Just a puppet, a plain old puppet.
Slowly the light fades away.
The puppet in a pretend world.
As the music slowly plays the last notes of the melody,
Lingering 'til the song has ended.
Only the puppet on a string remains.
Pull a string, watch me walk.
Pull another string, listen to me talk.

Chapter Twenty-Two

SOUL MATE

Say What?

My dearest,
I do not like you.
Say What?
I love you with all that I am.
My darling,
I do not need you.
Say What?
I want you.
My beloved,
I do not want to hug you.
Say What?
I want to devour and embrace all of you.
My husband,
I do not want to be just a wife.
Say What?
I want to be your best friend, your soul mate.
My Romantic lover,
I do not want to obey you.
Say What?
I want to honor you.
My dearest Daniel,
I am not protecting you when I do not say feelings.
Say What?
I will speak only the truth.
You are my man.
My Lover,
I do not want *sex*.
Say What?
I want to make *love* to my husband. My coach,
I am so in love with you.
I am yours, yesterday, today, and the tomorrows.
Say What?
I am yours through the end of end.
My husband,

We do not need a huge ceremony to exchange our vows.
Say What?
Our hearts are bonded with a happy ever after.

My married life was greeted with the love, kindness, and happiness. Shawn and I were married on his twenty-third birthday, October 9, 1983.

We married in Palm Desert, California. It was a nice, small wedding.

His family participated in the ceremony. Gus, Shawn's stepfather, was Shawn's best man. Maryann, who was married to Shawn's friend, little Shawn, was my bridesmaid.

Standing in front of the pastor and hearing the vows spoke to our hearts, we held each other's hands, listening to the words of each sentence of God's Vows to be with each other.

Shawn's little sister, who was two years old, began wailing. She wanted to be up next to her brother. Then Shawn's grandfather hearing aid was humming. The sound was soft at first, but with no warning, the humming echoed in the chapel.

"'Til death do you part." Those words sounded like a boom from the *heavens*.

I released the words, "'Til death do you part."

I looked at Shawn, who was serious, answering the pastor's questions.

"I do!" he said very loudly.

I felt the laughter explode in my throat. The noise rose in my throat, laughing with each symbol.

"Do you, Crystal Dawn White, take Shawn Neil Golston as your wedded husband?"

"Yes. I do!"

The laughter was uncontrolled able. I backed off the stage and rushed to the door leading out of the chapel. I thought I was existing the chapel; instead, I entered the bathroom There was no window, no escape.

I pulled myself together, and with my courage to face the question from Shawn and the family, I stood next to Shawn.

"Should I start over?" the pastor asked.

"No. Please continue were you left off."

I could feel Shawn's hurt fill my heart.

The ceremony was finished.

Shawn pulled me aside and asked, "What happened?"

I explained my nervousness and the sounds from both his grandfather and sister. I laughed. This was not how I pictured my wedding to be.

The pastor asked if we would like a photo of this special day.

Shawn held the back of my blouse. He was still angry. He was afraid I would leave again.

We were married for thirty-two years. Shawn left this world, a part of me left with him too. We stayed friends, partners and soul—mates together in our marriage, in our lives, enduring the roller coaster of marriage. We had humor throughout our marriage.

I asked Shawn on several occasions if we could redo our wedding ceremony. Every anniversary, same answer—*no.*

On our tenth anniversary, Shawn surprised me with a wedding ceremony. His family decorated the restaurant, and our sons kept silent with the secret of marrying, redoing our vows.

"Mom, Dad said that you should get really dressed up for dinner. Your friend, TJ, will drive you to the restaurant since Dad will be getting out of work later than he thought."

I dressed in a formal black dress. TJ drove me to the restaurant.

It looked closed. The lights were off. David, Shawn's boss, greeted me at the entrance of the restaurant.

"Looks like rolling blackouts." I wondered why David was here.

He seemed to know I was curious.

"Shawn asked if me and Susan could take the boys for the night." That sounded like Shawn.

David escorted me through the restaurant. No lights were on. Then, as if on cue, the walk path to the tables were lightened with trees and floral arrangements. The chairs lined the path, where guests have been seated.

In the front row were friends who worked in the police force.

Shawn was standing under the altar decorated with red roses.

"Here is your *bride.*"

David took my arm and placed it onto Shawn's arm. With a swift kiss on my cheek, David backed away onto Shawn's left side.

I Am so Tired of Trying

I pleaded with God, take me instead.
It was supposed to be me. I was to be taken…not my *beloved*…
Shawn, you were always the strong one.
You conquered mountains and swam the deepest oceans.
I am so tired of trying.
In my mind and heart, I am so lost.
My nights, I am alone. Shadows play in my dreams.
Shawn, you are gone.
You are lost, and I am empty.
I am so tired of trying.
I am so blue, so terribly cold.
Shawn, you promised we would grow old in each other's arms.
I am so tired of trying.
The day that God brought you home, my beloved left me.
I prayed, "Take me instead."
I felt the pain. I felt the sorrow.
Now, I feel the loneliness.
Give Shawn *peace*.
It should have been me.
I am so tired of trying.
Did I wish Shawn away?
Did I cause Shawn to leave?
I am pleading, Shawn, stay with me.
Please, do not *go*…
Hold *on*…
I need you.
I am so tired of trying.
I listen to music.
I listen to the lyrics.
Each word describes our *love*.
You are my *heart*.
My tears fall with sadness.
I am so tired of trying.
Thank you for the last weeks we spent together.

God granted me time and memories with my beloved. Now I am
one...
I begged for a few more minutes to hold, love, and cradle my beloved.
I am so tired of trying.
I feel weak, tired, and empty.
I want to go home with you.
I want to be in my beloved's arms once again.
I am so tired of trying.
Take me with you, Shawn.
I want to continue our journey.
Our destiny has only begun.
Our hearts are still beating as one.
I feel so alone, take me with you.
I am so tired of trying.
Take me home.
I am so alone.
So scared of what could have been.
I just need you near.
I cannot fight this anymore.
I want to come home.
I am so tired of trying.
One night of loneliness.
There are no dreams.
I can only cry, the tears feel like daggers in my *heart*.
I am so tired of trying.
I have a hole in my *heart*.
I no longer want to live.
This is a new chapter to write...new characters, new scenes, new life.
I am so tired of trying.
After thirty-two years of marriage.
My life is so empty, so distant...
I hear your voice, and yet I hear nothing, but the heartbeat is only
one.
I am so tired of trying.
You were my beginning and my end.
"Where are you tonight?"

You are not in my dreams!
"Why did you start this journey solo?"
"Will you come to me?"
I am so tired of trying.
Shawn, I want to come home.
I do not want to be alone.
"Where is your smile?"
The twinkle in your eyes...
"Where is my knight in shining armor?"
"Where is my soulmate?"
My heart weeps for my darling, my love...
I am so tired of trying.
Is it time to stop the clock?
Is it time to reach the boat dock?
I been waiting for the new sunrise,
To start a new beginning.
You promised me a future.
Now I travel this path by myself.
There is no rhyme or reason.
I am so tired of trying.
Your dreams were mine.
Take me home, my love.
I cannot do this alone.
I am so tired of trying.

September 10, 2014

Chapter Twenty-Three

DEAR DADDY

January 21, 2010

Dear Daddy,

Last night I felt terror in my thoughts. I could feel the panic in my heart. I woke from a heartbreaking dream. Tears are filling my eyes, escaping to my face. My head, throbbing like crushed waves, smashing, violently upon the rocks, the undertow grabbing my soul, the sand, and my body beating against the boat docks.

The fear of losing you and all the lost years of not being in your life, the tormenting nightmares.

Dad, I may not have the ability to make time rewind, and the past can be changed.

Perhaps this is why I am the person I am today.

The past is what it is…

I fear that I will not be the daughter you would be proud of.

I need you very much.

I need my father to protect me.

Be my warrior, keep the demons from the past, stay buried.

The horrific memories are creeping into my everyday life, my thoughts. A smell, touch, or even a word fills me with terror.

Dad, I know you were not able to protect me as a child.

You were always laboring, keeping food and a roof above your family's head. I know you craved this same comfort as me.

I wrote this letter to my dad before we drove to Cody, Wyoming, in 2009. We were headed to see Mark at the address, 9 Dogwood Road, Cody, where my father and mother lived. Mark moved in the residence November 2008. During Thanksgiving 2009, just me and Dad came to Cody, Wyoming, to finish with court probate and make sure Mark and his girlfriend were taking care of the property, etc.

Dad, I also know you did everything in your power to give your family the security of a good home life. Or as you thought.

I wanted to *yell* from the hilltops, this was my father.

I love you, *Dad*. I never want to lose your love. I need you so much. I need your wisdom, your strength, but most of all, I need to be able to talk with you.

Some subjects will be extremely hard to have a conversation about. I need you to hear me, understand the pain and sadness that has filled my heart.

I know now you are not a strong man to go against Mother. But I did not realize this 'til I was an adult. As a child, you destroyed my belief that you could protect me. I was left alone, *no adult* to protect me.

I need to explain the situation, situations that have and are invading my life as a mother, wife, and daughter.

I went to discuss the *abuse* with a therapist. Going through several avenues to conquer the darkness I been keeping secret in my mind.

I have several questions, and I am not sure if or can answer. The subjects are very sensitive. I am hoping you may be able to fill in the blanks.

Dad, I feel I failed as a mother and wife.

I also feel I failed as a daughter.

Dad, I am afraid of Mark. He is very capable of hurting, or worse, killing you and me.

Dad, please do not hate me! I never wanted to bring sadness into your heart.

I wished I could unburden my soul and heart upon you. I would love to be able to discuss and enjoy what time is left in our future.

Dad, you're my world. Shawn and I have dreams to be in your future. We would like to retire, spend time with you, listen to your stories, your love of the cowboy world.

I would stay with you in Wyoming, while Shawn finished his semester in college.

I would enjoy and love spending time with my father. God has granted us a chance to reconnect. We are on borrowed time.

Children are a gift. They are a loan from the *heavens*.

I know my sons are precious to me. I would be forever grateful to be in their lives 'til my death.

I would never trade our talks. I found a little peace and knowledge with you.

Thank you, *Dad*. You are worth all the *gold diamonds* and *money* in the world.

I have heard your voice, I have seen your eyes, I have seen your smile, I have enjoyed your laughter.

I praise you for giving life.

I regret that so many years have been stolen and the past cannot be changed. The future is all that is left.

With each breath and heartbeat, I am learning and finding inner peace to forgive
You!

Love you. Crystal D. Golston

I do not want to go into details at this time.

I beg you to remain by my side. Since I am coming to your aide. Making sure that the probate with the courts, and estate is taken care of, with you always in mind.

Shawn is not able to join us back to Cody, Wyoming. He is not feeling well. He did speak to you about me.

Mark followed me outside the front door.

The smoke from the burned dinner and the cigs was toxic. I stayed on the porch. At this time Mark stated I am not welcomed at your home. Mark said he is taking care of your finances and that I was not allowed to go through the property. If I wanted anything, I was to inform him. I was given three days, and after that, I was not going to be allowed on the property.

I went into the bedroom that was yours, at the far end of the house. I was expecting you to also stay in that room as well. I placed an air mattress for me, and you use your bed.

Mark and Barb slept in your mother's bedroom.

Instead of staying nearby, you went to the travel trailer and slept there.

During the night, Mark came into the bedroom I was sleeping in. I even placed a sitting chair under the bedroom doorknob. This did not restrain him from intruding my sleep.

After threatening him with bodily and financial devastation, he left the room, but not before terrorizing me with assault, like from my childhood.

The reason I was determined about leaving the following day was the fear of him killing me.

I have carried the *blame*, the *shame*, and the *secrets*.

Am I responsible for the *misery! Sadness!* and your disapproval of *me* as your blood *daughter?*

I prayed that you would love me.

I prayed that you would be my savior, from mother, and my brothers.

I carried the shame of Mark's perverted hate.

I carried the blame of Mother's abuse.

I carried the secret, of your closed eyes.

The eyes that did witness the assaults and the cruel abuse.

Dad, I am extremely concerned that you would again turn your back on me. Am I correct? Even after twenty-seven years to remain out of your life until I was notified that Mother died.

Twenty-seven years I remained away from both of you.

Mother's jealously was not of a loving mother, but of a female. Her jealously became violent and extremely violent as I grew older.

Couple of years prior to mother's death, I began researching my mother's parental linage.

I found more secrets.

After we went to Cody for Thanksgiving, it was about a year after mother's death. Maybe a little more than a year since mother's death.

Her passing.

I was uneasy with Mark in your home. He had a new girlfriend and involved with a biker club.

I begged you not leave me alone with Mark by myself. I even explained why.

Richard Anson White Sr., Cody, Wyoming, 2009

Richard Anson White Sr., Cody, Wyoming, 2008

Handprint of Child

Sometimes you get discouraged
Because I am so small
And always leave my fingerprints
On furniture and wall
But everyday I'm growing up
And soon I'll be so tall
That all those little handprints
Will be so hard to recall
So here's a final handprint
Just so that you can say
This is how my fingers looked
1970 on Christmas Day

Chapter Twenty-Four

COMEDY OR TRAGEDY

I do not know if I will ever hear or see my grandchildren.

I do not know if I will hear them call me *Grandma* or feel their kisses, their hugs.

I do not know if this is my last sunrise; each day that I breath is either a *blessing* or a *curse*.

Watching my son's grow into young men has been a gift from *Our Lord Jesus Christ*. I hear their voices, I feel their kisses, and love their hugs.

The encouragement from my sons and my husband during this trial of hardships is a *blessing* as well.

The difference between wanting to live or die.

The days I felt like a burden, like I have no purpose. "What is my purpose?" "What do I exist for?" "Is my life worth anything?"

Then in the next second, I listen to my inner voice, "*God* would never waste, a breath, a heartbeat, nor a soul!" I know I have a purpose!

I am not a poker player, but I know that I was dealt a *wild card* It is up to me to either *fold* or *gamble* with the cards I am holding.

I place all my poker chips into the *tomorrows*. Although I have to endure the *pain*, the *endless nights* of tormented restless muscle cramps, burning nerve pain, or the twisted spasms from the creeping invasion into my body. *Lupus.* My body was held hostage by a phantom of mental anguish.

I know I have to find an *ace* in this poker hand of cards.

The challenge of finding another creative way to hide my developing disabilities.

Again, I am staring into the mirror, searching for the woman who I was, who was confident and had self-worth. Instead, I saw my reflection, no longer had strength; no longer attractive. That woman has disappeared into the abyss.

The woman I was months ago now moved slower. Stiffness has crept into my body. My bones, nerves, and skin have been replaced by an *alien*.

Is this the same woman that worked in the hospitality workforce? Who can no longer raise her arms to style her hair? The tailored garments no longer fit. High heels that was part of the uniform, I used to walk with *pride*.

Now! It is a hazard. I put my makeup on with every detail perfect. I was a positive role model. That woman has disappeared too.

I tell myself, "You could feel pity, feel sorry for yourself. No one would blame me" or "I could find a purpose, something that has meaning. Make my life more than an existence. Not let the illness control me." But what? What is my purpose?

I decided to make a new chapter in my life., I could either write my own ending or let the *demon* of despair, of hate, disgust, make my story, my ending. So what is my *existence*? I have no choice, yet fear of failure remains in the back of my mind. But truth failure is only if I do not try. I might fall down. I will just have to pick myself up off the ground. Start over again and again. My story is not finished. I am only in the middle of my life.

My chronic illness is a roller coaster. Never knowing if the next day will be a *good* day or a *bad* day. I learned not to plan or schedule activities. Day by day became my pledge.

I also learned about prejudice. If an employee has become ill with a chronic disability, either physical or mental illness, it is a stressful situation during most work environments. The level of stress placed on a person who is in management, the level of stress is extremely high already. The tasks will be examined very closely and scrutinized. The high standards of production, there is no place for failure, nor excuses. I already placed enormous tasks upon myself. I needed to prove I am capable and could complete each task to the highest level of standards beyond that is expected from other employees. There could not be any doubt in the higher level of management I am capable and would complete my tasks without interruptions due to my body deterioration.

I would push myself harder and longer than a well and fit person could do.

Truth, my employer did not care about how much I applied or had success in keeping the profits high, low employee hours on several shifts or tasks. Nor how to keep moral and grooming standards during functions, like banquets for celebrities and government officials, etc. while managing other departments in the *hotel business*. The only important thing that my employer was interested in was the hours maintained to a low minimum, which I did do for two months, six days a week, twelve hours a day, especially on salary.

I became stressed even more, and my illness flared; it was noticeable. The fatigue and lack of sleep made the flare-ups from *lupus* extremely painful.

I was having difficulties at least a couple of hours during my shifts. I still worked between ten to twelve hours a day.

Every stage I managed to climb over or around my illness was a *victory,* a *triumph.* I truly believed in *me!*

Yes! I have *good* and *bad* days!

I question myself on good days, "Am I all right? Why am I feeling fine?" Because on my really *bad* days, it is brutal. I felt the worst pains and exhaustion, trying to prove to myself that I was capable of doing housework chores, maintaining a stable home environment. I did not ask for *bad* days, but I know those bad days were around the corner. I prayed for *good* days, each morning when I wake up, it will either be a *great day!* Which I praise *Our Lord Jesus Christ* for giving me another painless day to enjoy my family. I enjoyed the beauty, which appeared every day outside my windows. I would put every chore, every task into this good day. I pushed my limits to accomplish tasks. *Why?* I know in a few hours I will not be able to finish. I would remain in bed for several hours or even days. Physically, I know no matter what I have accomplished or not able to complete, I at least have tried to stay useful. I will give every ounce and every drop of blood. I will stay positive, even with an *alien*…named *lupus*.

Without bad days, I feel like a part of me is missing. *Lupus* could either be my destroyer or my blessing. I chose blessing! *Why?* I know I will never be rid of this illness. I can, however, give others encouragement. Find the shelf and put in a box, ribbon, and wrap. My illness had a label. I did not want it to control my life. I have learned to manage the illness. Those good days, I take advantage of those days. The bad days—I rest and rebuild my strength. I am able to accomplish the tasks a little easier.

I want to spend quality time with my sons. I will and have during the days I rested also the good days.

I wish perhaps my story will be uplifting and know they are not alone. Use mind over matter to your best ability.

Chapter Twenty-Five

MIKHEAL, GUARDIAN ANGEL

I have questioned myself if Mikheal was my guardian Angel.

Or was he my imaginary friend?

I honestly believe Mikheal is my guardian angel.

First time I knew Mikheal was guarding me, I was about a year and half years old.

I was crying and holding my stuff toy (a poodle dog).

My mother and her friend, Dick, were visiting other friends in Powell, Wyoming.

We stayed the night at mother's friends while Mother and Dick drank beer and played cards all night. Mother instructed me and my brothers to sleep on the folded-out couch made into bed.

During the night, I needed to use the bathroom. I tried holding it as long as possible. I felt a warmth liquid soaking through bedding and mattress. Midmorning, Mother and Dick woke up. Mother told JR to take me to the bathroom. Mother noticed my nightgown, and the bedding was wet.

Mother spanked and scolded me. Showing Dick what I had done, she said, "Are you *lazy*? Why didn't you use the bathroom?" Of course, I had no answer. Mother said, "Do not move from this couch."

I obeyed. I feared Mother would be angry if I woke her. Dick carried me to the wood shed. He carefully chose a tree limb and swatted my butt. Afterward, I was tossed onto the couch/bed.

My mother yanked me with a jolt. "Do not be *lazy* again!"

"Do not move from this couch!" Sitting in a wet puddle, my clothes dried, I smelled of urine.

I felt a warm, comforting touch. My head rested in safe arms, Mikheal's arms! His voice, soft, and soothing, a melody tone.

In my ear he said, "You are *loved*. Every day is a blessing. You are my sweet and dear *angel*."

Mikheal appeared with beautiful, glittering white wings. The wings folded around my stained face. My tears Mikheal wiped away with a tender touch. I could feel Mikheal's touch lingering after he moved his fingers, the impression of his enduring kisses and cradling my head.

Mikheal's words were as tender as his touch, "I shall never leave. You are my *heart*." Mikheal put my hand on his chest. "You and I are entwined."

"Our hearts are placed together." I could not understand Mikheal's meaning of his words that he spoke. I did understand Mikheal's smile, his safe arms, and knowing I was not alone.

Mickeal has been true to his promise. Mikheal has not left my side. Mikheal cannot *stop* the *abuse!* Mikheal showed me *love, kindness*, and brought me out of my darkness.

Mikheal wiped away my tears. He gave me encouragement, keeping my heart beautiful. My *faith* has been challenged and trials of confusion all through my years of life. Mikheal always reminded me *God* has not forgotten his lamb of innocents. *God* has not forgotten *me!*

I am loved. I am worthy. No breath or heartbeat is a waste.

Devil loves chaos. He loves sadness, and most of all, he wants more demons to carry on the legacy of bringing absolute *evil*.

Mikheal showed his *love, support, and heart*.

God placed a *guardian angel* to show me the goodness and *faith* of decent people.

Several times in my past I tried to end the pain, guilt, and blame. I was forced to shield the shame as mine.

This is not my *secret* to keep.

I am not to blame.

Message to My Angel

Message to my angel.
Are you listening?
Do you hear me?
The day I knew you were real,
December 1965.
Our eyes locked, our hearts
We are contacted from the *heavens*
Through the clouds.
You are my guardian angel.

You protect and comfort me.
Now the time is near, my life will disappear.
You hold me so dear.
Message to my angel.
Are you listening?
Do you hear me?
I took your hand with gentle kisses
You placed on my head.
Your eyes spoke to mine,
Only tears and sadness.
Time to leave this world, be in mine.
Your love and kindness, no more madness.
Message to my angel.
Are you listening?
Do you hear me?
Your addiction is no more.
Your confliction has left you with sores.
Miles will separate the sadness.
Remember only the smiles.
Heaven is where you belong.
Tell this cruel world, so long.
Message to my angel.
Are you listening?
Do you hear me?
My angel's voice sounds with a melody.
I promise you, you are mine.
I will spend my life time making up for lost.
Your heart was the cost.
You will never part.
The Lord has given you a new start.
Message to my angel.
Are you listening?
Do you hear me?
I was promised our Lord, wings of angel.
The heavens comfort me.
The Lord's embrace is so strong.

The Lord's love is never wrong.
Message to my Angel.
Are you listening?
Do you hear me?

July 07, 1982

Chapter Twenty-Six

LOOKING INTO MY SOUL

I know my strength is because of my *faith*. I have questioned myself, "*What is faith?*"

"What do I have *faith* in?"

My answer is, Lord Jesus Christ! I know, in the darkest part of my life, God never left my side. I am the one who left *God* behind.

After I left my dungeon in 1982, I built another dungeon inside myself. I blamed myself for the shame and secrets I carried in my heart. Feeling that everything that has or had happened in my past, childhood was my fault.

Truth, I had no control over other people's thoughts, actions, nor their judgment. I wanted and needed everyone to like me. I adapted and change myself to fit into that bowed, wrapped box and kept on a shelf inside my protected mind. I believed people I wanted in my life, I had to change my perceptive to have their approval. My ideas of adapting to other's needs continued through my early adulthood, between my twenties into my early thirties and again in my forties. Only until now in my fifties.

I actually began feeling whole for the first time. With the love, kindness, and trusted friendship with *Kim Asay*. Kim has shown me a wonderful Christian devotion and unconditional friendship. I have a sister of hearts. Kim is a true gift from *God*.

April 2017 I fell in love with a wonderful and handsome gentleman. He has given me strength, support, and honesty. Our relationship bloomed into soul mate. Dan had a heart of gold. His smile created a wholesome bond of friendship, kinship, into a love. The bond our hearts created is filled with happiness, joy, and security. Daniel gives me unconditional love, no strings, no ties, only pure love from his whole being.

Daniel is my second chance to feel life, feel a strong bond of happiness. We will spend our vintage years with passion, enjoying *God's* creation.

I will *speak up!*

I will speak, I will see, I will hear.

I am no longer going to be *silent*.

Daniel has brought my inner self to the surface. Our relationship is bonded with respect of each other's thoughts, beliefs, and loyalty to each other.

Within my first marriage to Shawn of thirty-two years, I slipped further away from my relationship to our Lord.

Looking back into my past, I came into the realization I did not make time or make room in my life for *God*. I truly needed *God* more than ever in my life, especially during my marriage, motherhood, and my adulthood. As a widow, I knew as long as there is a church standing, I needed to bring the Lord Jesus Christ into my world. I never seemed to have time for *God*. I needed the truth, the structure, and the sanctuary that was between the church walls. I needed *God!*

I started to believe that there were imitations of *God*. This was the *devil* speaking to my heart and *soul*.

I started to take a deeper look at my inner self, the damaged and broken Crystal; the young child that needed to be held, loved, and treated with tender loving arms. *Unconditional love!*

Do I have to be indebted to a minster, pastor, or preacher?

I only needed to feel *God's love*.

How would I ever trust religion? My mother used religion as a tool to enlist her faults, her demon that fed on a child's fear.

My mother spoke like she was a Christian. Yet she was a perfect specimen of the *devil's spawn*. Mother used religion as an instrument for discipline. She would find verses out of the *Bible* to inflict fear and pain upon my body, soul, and heart. The punishment would be as it was written in the Bible verse.

For instance, in the Bible, Proverbs 13:24, "Those who spare the rod of discipline hate their children. Those who love their children care enough to discipline them."

Mother would use the verse from the Bible Deuteronomy 21:20–21: This son of ours is stubborn and a rebellious and refuses to obey. He is a glutton and a drunkard. Then all the men of his town must stone him to death, this way you purge this evil from among you, and all Israel will hear about it and be afraid.

Mother used religion as a tool to enforce her evilness.

Faith and belief were only adhered in my childhood and my youth. I lost my faith between eighteen and fifty-two years of age.

My excuse, my reasoning for discarding my faith? I was tearing away the *Word of God* because I felt God had turned away from me. I was very wrong!

Why would *God* allow those who pretended to be Christians be ignorant and not interfere in my family secrets, *abuse, emotional, physical, sexual? Where was God?*

A *God* who I believed would, should, and could protect me against the *evil* human beings, who caused my scars deeper than just skin wounds.

Where was God during my childhood?

Why did he remain *silent?*

I started doubting Jesus's promises. His word fell on deaf ears, just like my abuser's cruel tormenting, paralyzing *abuse* fell silent on *deaf ears too.*

I doubted God's mercy.

I doubted Mikheal, my guardian angel.

Most of all, I *doubted me.*

I had no self-esteem.

I *had* no self-worth.

I took credit and blamed failures of others. I disconnected from relationships. My appearance contributed to the lack of confidence. My lack of the passion to life, inadequacies, and my inner peace was the hinder of quality see myself as a woman of worth, a mother who was loved by her sons. Yet I felt that I did not deserve to be loved. I was not worthy of such an honor to give unconditional love to or from a child.

The lack of finding myself in anyone's heart, no strings, no ties, just to be loved for *me.*

I learned to perceive my mother's excessive emotional and ver-bal *abuse* as intertwined and rooted itself into my thoughts. *Negative* and *ugly* words created the woman that I had become: *unworthy, useless,* and *undeserving love.*

My attention always focused on the negative inadequacies of my physical form. I would examine my appearance with anguish and distaste, which had distracted the positive definitions of my body, mind, and heart. *No value.*

My energy evaluated that my self-worth was in my appearance and not self-worth.

I have not been able to escape the pain, torture, and the faded bruises still obvious today, as if the scars were placed upon my body yesterday. My scars continued to inflect myself because I only knew hate, distain, and cruelty.

I am not worthy of being loved!

My relationship within myself, my inner soul, was continually plagued with negative addiction, self-destructive behavior.

I asked myself, "What will make you happy? Just a little happiness and joy in your world? What was or is *happiness?*" My answer—being a good mother!

In 2017 my journey began upward, out of the depths of darkness. Placing a shroud around myself, I was always afraid of being hurt or injured by anyone or someone I trusted with my heart!

My illusion—I could manage my life, my heart, and my process of dealing with trauma, reoccurring frightening nightmares, and the insanity of my childhood dysfunctional family dynasty.

I believe *God* is infinite. I am his daughter. My knowledge of the Bible is not only written words on a page. It is God's promises.

I was extremely ignorant. I did not have the presence of mind to have *faith*, let alone to understand the true meaning of God's words. I did not have the capacity to feel *faith*. I believed that since I did not see *God*, nor did I see evidence of *God* in a human form, therefore, I did not believe God existed.

I was so *wrong!*

My thoughts needed to be pure, no doubts or questioning *God's* promises and his words. God promised to bring justice, and only God could punish the ones who inflicted *evil* upon the innocent children, disabled people, and injured souls. God promised to fulfill the legacy promised to our forefathers.

I only needed to listen, feel, and keep a pure understanding with my *heart* and *soul.* I needed a humble *heart.*

God is the ultimate *power!*

God is the *voice* of *splendor!*
God created *me!*
My strength came from *God!*
I am a *survivor!*

If I did not believe this, or knew that I am a survivor, I would not be here on *earth* at this exact moment.

I learned to adapt to certain situations and remain under the radar. Stay out of sight. Stay hidden.

My self-esteem and self-worth was influenced by my image or reflection in the mirror.

Crystal Dawn Gorton-White-Golston, thirty-two years old, Palm Springs, California

Chapter Twenty-Seven

MODELING AND BEAUTY PAGEANTS

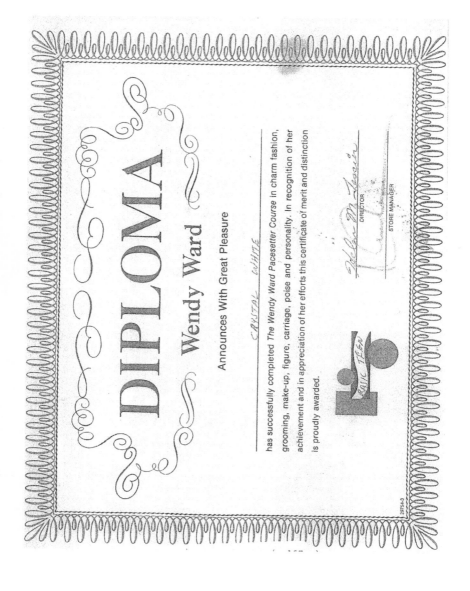

DIPLOMA

Wendy Ward

Announces With Great Pleasure

CRYSTAL WHITE

has successfully completed *The Wendy Ward Pacesetter Course* in charm fashion, grooming, make-up, figure, carriage, poise and personality. In recognition of her achievement and in appreciation of her efforts this certificate of merit and distinction is proudly awarded.

DIRECTOR

STORE MANAGER

PAVIL TEEN

29754-3

240

Wendy Ward Charm Studio

"Every girl has beauty potential, and the Wendy Ward staff of professional charm and modeling instructors want to help you find your individual "key to beauty" through personal attention and analysis and the experience of gaining poise through modeling and participation in the many events planned exclusively for our students.

It's never too late to join the world of beauty, grace and confidence. Mail the attached card or call your local Wendy Ward for more information, reservations. All seats reserved prior to 1st meeting.

PLEASE ADDRESS THE ENROLLMENT
CARD TO THE MONTGOMERY WARD
STORE NEAREST YOU

Los Angeles Area Montgomery Ward Stores are
located at:

Canoga Park	
Topanga Plaza	883-1000
Costa Mesa	
3088 Bristol	549-9400
Covina	
Barranca at San Bernardino Freeway	966-7411
Eagle Rock	
2826 Colorado Blvd.	254-9261
Fullerton	
Harbor at Orangethorpe	879-2500
Hawthorne	
1200 Hawthorne Blvd.	970-7305
Huntington Beach	
Edinger at Beach Blvd.	892-6611
Lakewood	
5252 Pepperwood Ave	633-7600
Lynwood	
Imperial Blvd. at State	537-6000
Montclair	
9050 Central Ave	621-3054
Norwalk	
Imperial at Norwalk Blvd.	868-0911
Panorama City	
Tobias at Roscoe	894-8211
Riverside	
3530 Riverside Plaza	784-3000
Rosemead	
Rosemead Blvd. at San Bernardino Fwy.	573-3110
San Bernardino	
Central City Mall	884-9231
Santa Ana	
Bristol at Seventeenth	547-6841
Torrance	
Del Amo Fashion Square	542-6971
West Los Angeles	
La Cienega at 18th St.	836-7922

Lecture and Fashion Show Service

Free lectures may be arranged on any subject within the beauty, fashion and modeling fields. Fashion Shows coordinated by Wendy Ward are available for schools and organizations.

☐ ⑦Please enroll me in your next class series. I understand I will be contacted soon to confirm my reservation.

☐ Check enclosed confirms my reservation.

☐ ⑦Plan on adding to my Ward's Charg-All account.

☐ ⑦Please add my name to your mailing list or upcoming class sessions.

Name *Crystal Sheer*

Address *1223 Cruifton Ave.*

City *Riverside Natofiti*

Zip *9174* Phone *330-2149*

School *Williams Bush Lett.*

Grade *9th* Age *14*

Tuition is due the 1st day of class

(168)

241

Meet the Academy's Director

Qualifications: Lyle Spilman JR has a solid and more extensive background than most when it comes to teaching professional acting and helping to shape theatric careers. *Examples*: For twelve and a half years, he was a State Licensed and Union Franchiser Theatrical Agency Owner and artist's manager. In this capacity, he worked with various theatrical unions, film, television studios, night clubs, conventions, plus handling and booking professional performers on the West Coast. He was hired and worked as talent director two years for Cinema Television Productions, a company that, through their written contracts, furnished the models for all the National Television Commercials for the Ford Motor Company.

Education: Although a Theatrical Arts and Film major at East Los Angeles City College, Pasadena City College, The Pasadena Playhouse, and UCLA, he also studied at several professional drama schools in Beverly Hills and Hollywood such as Ben Bards, The Actor's Lab, Gellors Workshop, and Anna Roache.

Hobbies: For eighteen years he worked in Summer Stock and Little Theatre, acting, directing, producing, organizing, setting up, and teaching acting workshops throughout Los Angeles and Orange Counties. He has directed more than sixty-three act plays plus many one acts, musicals, and variety shows.

Other qualifications: The past eleven years he has worked fulltime in the Beauty Pageant field on local, state, and national levels with practically every major program, which includes Miss International, Junior Miss, Miss Teen Age America, Miss Universe, Miss America, and Mrs. USA Homemaker. For two and a half years he was the state executive director and producer of the Miss California, Miss Nevada, and Miss Hawaii pageants for the Miss World Pageant of London, England. In this capacity, he worked directly with the Bob Hope Overseas Christmas shows.

He created and directed his own patriotic program, the Miss Liberty USA Pageant—now in its tenth year of existence. This program has won a National Freedom's Foundation Award from Valley Forge and has written endorsements from state legislators, US congressmen, senators, Former Governor Reagan, and Former Presider Nixon.

Method of instruction: Due to his background, he is automatically programed to only one method of instruction. That is to prepare the student to become a working professional and to then be able to earn their living in the entertainer industry. Thus, his classes are not to be confused with that of a babysitter or a place to "kill" a little extra time. The classes start and end on time.

Each student must be prepared to "work" during the entire class period.

Question: What is to be gained by those who seek this instruction and then later decides not to enter the field of show business?

Answer: There will be many important gains to be enjoyed and utilized throughout that student's life. Brief examples: *Poise, self-confidence, the ability to stand tall at any given time and speak properly, whether it be in front of two or two thousand people. Also learning how to think, look, and seek.*

MISS U.S.A. LIBERTY
BEAUTY PAGEANT
AWARD

𝕿𝖔 _____ Crystal D. White _____

1st. Annual "Petite and Little Miss
Liberty USA" Beauty Pageant
Contestant

In appreciation of the active assistance given
to the Miss U.S.A. Liberty Pageant in
furthering the life work of preserving
our American Heritage

244

MISS U.S.A. LIBERTY BEAUTY PAGEANT AWARD

To *Crystal White*
Junior Teen Senior Finals
School.

2nd ANNUAL
PETITE AND LITTLE
Miss Liberty USA Pageant Finals
Sunday, September 26, 1976 — 2:00 and 6:00 p.m.

ROSEMEAD HIGH SCHOOL AUDITORIUM
Just north of Valley on Rosemead Boulevard
City of Rosemead

DONATION: $1.00

tance given
grant in
serving

weekend in Hacienda Heights.

HACIENDA HEIGHTS TEENS practice walking gracefully as they prepare for yet another beauty pageant where hopefully one of these gals will walk off, gracefully of course, with the crown. Seen practicing are left to right, Crystal White, Meg Mitchell with the book on her head, and Christy Willis making sure Meg is standing straight and tall.

(Photos by Rich Lipski)

dreams that come true.

In our community, there are some of these girls that want to wear the crown, hear the crowds cheer, and walk down the ramp, to the music . . . one step at a time. They are trained to walk tall, erect, but with spirit. These girls have been working these last years to get to the top, to wear the crown.

Some of the girls pictured here, have received a crown or two — Debby Love is Junior Miss of California in the Liberty Pageant. Shellye Dean has appeared in the Dr. Pepper Junior Teen Pageant and was a runner-up . . .

The girls will compete this coming Sunday in the Miss Walnut Valley Show. The winners there, will go on to the Orange Show in Riverside next month and then on to State finals.

Appearing in bathing suit competition, formal attire, and pantsuits, they will be judged for looks, composure, how they handle themselves, charm, beauty and most important of all the ability to communicate the desire to be a winner.

The show is open to the public and will be h Hacienda Heights Wo Club and there is an sion charge of

Judges for the show will include Mary Bewald active in pageant work and Director of the Southern California Pageant for 15 years, Marice Mount Director of Miss East Los Angeles County Pageant also involved in beauty pageant work for many years, and George sen, Director Riverside

Beauty Pageant Newspaper Article: Miss Walnut Valley

The HIGHLANDER

January 5, 1977

DIFFICULT CHOICE.....Judges at the Jan. 16 Miss Walnut Valley Beauty Pageant will have a difficult time selecting title winners from among many talented contestants, including (l-r) Denise Doyle, Christy Willis, Crystal White, Diana Whitehead and Debby Love.

Local Beauties To Compete For Crown

HACIENDA HEIGHTS – The first annual Junior, Teenage and Senior "Miss Walnut Valley" Beauty Pageant has been scheduled for Sunday, Jan. 16, in the Hacienda Heights Women's Clubhouse.

Young women between the ages of 12 and 24 who are single, have never been married or had children.

are eligible to compete for trophies, ribbons, crowns and the opportunity to participate in other pageants. There will also be a special competition for petite and little girls ages 6 through 11.

The newly crowned "Senior Miss Walnut

Valley" will spend three all expense paid days, along with a chaperone, competing against forty-nine other reigning city and area queens for the title of National Citrus Queen in San Bernardino, March 17. The winner there receives a two-week all expense paid

trip to New Zealand as a special guest of that government.

Newspaper Article: The beauty pageant I participated in—Miss Walnut; Crystal Dawn White, Beauty Pageant, Hacienda Heights, California, 1977

247

Beauty Pageant, Crystal Dawn White,
Miss. Liberty, age eleven years

Crystal Dawn White, age fourteen years old
Photo taken by Dennis Chuchian

Modeling, Crystal Dawn White, age twelve years, getting ready for pageant, Diamond Bar, Hacienda Heights, California

Modeling, Crystal Dawn White, Los Angeles, California, 1980

CRYSTAL WHITE

1-13-77

Hi,

I really enjoyed taking pictures of Crystal at the photo center. She is such a pretty girl, and she looks great in pictures too.

I hope she keeps going to camera days this summer.

My negatives were not as sharp as I had hoped they would be. So five by seven is the largest standard size they could be enlarged. Before the unsharpness became a problem.

Hope to see you again soon.

Your friend,
Eric Kongs

Modeling 1977, Los Angeles, California

Modeling, Crystal
Dawn White,
Los Angeles,
California, 1980

Crystal White; *Actor*, Vincent Barbi, 1981

Chapter Twenty-Eight

EMOTIONS OF A SURVIVOR POEMS

Couple of Aces

A couple of aces, two people who will guide, create a safe place, always by your side.

A couple of aces, show you the path, when the journey is darkened, they lighten your walk.

A couple of aces, they hold your hand, comfort you, always close protecting you from the unknown.

A couple of aces, bring you joy and happiness, giving you the seeds to grow.

They share your triumphant and your defeats.

With tender kisses and love gives the encouragement to meet the next hurdles. No failures, no regrets, just victories.

A couple of aces, share your burden, carry the weight, 'til you are able to be victorious.

They take your pain, there is no shame. There is no blame.

They always keep you safe.

A couple of aces.

October 27, 1979

This Is My Fantasy of How I Wished My Parents Would Have Been to Me Sleepless Nights

I can only sit on my bed and read a story that I already read.

When I turn off the lights, I listen to the cool whispers of the quiet night.

I just lay watching the moon's shadows, creeping slowly over the silent meadows.

When I fall asleep, I am awakened by the night's quietness.

Only the morning light releases me. The sun appears, a brand-new day.

Oh, how many of these weary, sleepless nights do I have to count?

I find myself alone, wondering if I will find solace.

A tender touch, a loving arm to rock me to sleep.

Would I mumble his name?

Will I find peace cradled in his arms?
Do I have to wait to go to *heaven* before
I am released from this sadness?
I am searching for comfort, praying for silent night.

July 28, 1980

Where Now?

As the piano keys play, the music grows stronger and louder.
As the piano keys release the smooth notes softly into the air,
I float gently through the breeze. I am lifted higher and higher,
Each cord guiding me toward the sunlight.
But soon the music fades. Each note lowering me into my reality.
The major notes pounding my haunted soul.

August 30, 1980

Players

We break the hearts of the ones we hold dear.
We break the spirit of the ones we want to keep near.
We break the souls of our bodies. We pledge our innocence to evil.
But yet we survived the torments that blocked exists.
What remains are the supporting characters of the play.
There is no past, present, or future.
There is no script, no speeches; the only light that shines is the sadness of our demise.

September 26, 1981

The Broken Spirit

My heart has gone to sleep.
My pulse has ceased.
My mind has no memories.

My soul has no love.
My spirit has been broken.
My spirit has been destroyed.
My feelings are nothing.
My pain, my fear, my sorrow, no laughter.
My world has crashed, no pleading,
There is no yesterday, no today, no tomorrows.

Date: September 14, 1981

The Single Bed Rose

My single red rose,
Who is very charming and dear.
My single red rose has brought me love and happiness
For all those who come near.
My single red rose lives day by day in the footsteps of our Lord.
My single red rose glitters like the dew brought from *heaven*.
When my single red rose cries a tear, the soft petals leave an imprint.
My single red rose has only Angel to wipe away the faded colors.
With a gentle wipe with his wings, a final gesture to say *goodbye*.
My single red rose holds a secret it holds near to the *heart*.
Remaining silent 'til the next petal is released into the morning sunrise.
My single red rose, hold my heart, my soul, my life; only in time will heal.
The faded color, the dying petal brings a promise of a new day.

October 27, 1981

The Mime

Am I a blind fool?
No morals, no hate, no love.
I must hide from myself.
I do not want to face the truth.

So no one can see my pain, the hurt.
Tears fall like raindrops,
leaving puddles of shame,
lost dignity.
I have lost my compass.
There is no time, no direction.
Every love I hold on tightly,
so tightly to my heart.
My love is gone, no longer a dream,
but a reality, no longer in a fantasy.
How do I face the future?
I protect my heart,
my endless wandering into the abyss.
I do not want gems,
I do not want money.
I want to be loved, just be *loved*...

Reflections of My Mind

I look back, desperately trying to capture the love.
I held once, but now he is gone.
As I try to remember the way he looked,
All the memories are fading, his smiles,
His tender kisses, gentle caress.
He slipped through my hands so quickly.
No trace, no shadow, only his last goodbye.
The tears, so many tears, lingering on my face.
A shattered love, shattered heart.
Splitters are that remains.
The door of time has closed.
The door will not open again, never again.
Only one grain of sand, still the hourglass remains empty.

No More, Feeling Empty

The lonely nights have disappeared.
I am in your arms tonight.
Your hands holding mine.
No more crying myself to sleep.
I could hear you whisper in my ear,
"I am very near.
Sleep, my angel, my dear.
No harm will come your way.
I may be far,
Yet my heart is not.
My thoughts are here.
You will always be safe, my dear."

Chapter Twenty-Nine

MY MOTHER'S LETTERS TO ME

After my mother passed away for a heart attack on September 12, 20—

I was notified from the police detent in Indio, California.

I was able to go through her personal letters, and I found these returned-to-sender letters among her important files in the safe.

Does it change my feelings for her?

No! She had ever chance to make amends to her children and stop to cycle of abuse.

Do I feel she was making excuses?

Hell yes, I believe she was making excuses.

Do I forgive her?

Yes, not for her, but for my own heart.

My mother did not care what my heart, memories, or soul was dealing with, the conflicts I felt. I forgave my mother for *peace* and not carry the baggage of emotional despair. I forgave my mother for *me!* For my *future!* For my children.

Due to the abusive and dominating actions from my grandmother, Doris Brummett, and brutal verbal, physical, and hate toward my mother, my mother carried the torch to the next generation.

I blew out the torch and maintained a family unit, although I feared that I would carry the DNA that was in my bloodline.

I am aware every day that only I had the power and control to stop the cycle.

The cycle has *stopped* with me.

God did not let me down. My mother let me down.

I pray that my mother may have found the wisdom to forgive her mother as well.

> Dear daughter and family,
>
> I gave my mare to a ten-year girl to ride, as I no longer am able to ride. I am afraid to, as I will get hurt. I am not the person you used to see and do so many things and not be afraid, as now I am afraid of my own shadow, it seems. I don't know what to do about it.

I have two male pups left from my May litter and three pups from the August litter. I have got to get them advertised. They are regular labs and need to get a couple of my older females worked so that they mind. I was going to just use them for breeding, but I think that I am going to sell them. I am tired and can't get around to good, and with Dad going to be gone for a year or two, we decided that I need to sell the two girls. I have a yellow lab and a black female lab that I will sell as soon as I get them started in obedience. The chocolate male and yellow male, they were the May-11 litter.

Dad is going to fly home in about eight days, and I am trying to get as much done as I can. I will go through some receipts tonight and make up some meals for him. He has been living in an old '86 motor home out in the desert, not even a tree or cactus around for ahead for him. It even broke the thermometer. It has been staying right at 120 degrees where it is at. So I want him to have some good meals while he is here. He will or only be home about six days and then back to the Vegas area.

There is not really much to write about here. I would like to see you. It has been twenty or more years since I saw you. I am heavier. I did a no-no. I dyed my hair black, and does it ever look awful. I don't know how Dad is going to react. I need to dye it back to blond, but I am going to have to wait for a couple of weeks. It will be a shock to Dad when I meet at the airport.

Words of Wisdom:

It's amazing how much more reasonable your parents become when you get older.

Always go for the best and learn to settle for less, but only when it's absolutely necessary.

It's useless to worry about things you cannot change.

If the road you're traveling is too rocky, look for another path.

Friends appreciate in value much faster than any investment.

It's easy to forget that other people's egos are easily bruised.

Don't make waves just for the sake of watching them crash on the shore.

Well, it is time for me to feed all the dogs and get them fresh water. I have one in the house that I had her barker taken out. She is a wonderful dog, but she would bark, and I couldn't stand it. She loves bananas. I have to give her soft food, and I put her meds in it, as the pills are rough for her throat. I make them soft also. I'm afraid that she is going to become spoiled and not want to go back to her kennel. I have kept her in the house for another ten days to be sure that nothing goes wrong. She is my best dog, or I should say, one of my best.

Well, honey, I will sign off for now, as I am sure you are becoming bored with this letter.

Remember, we love you.

Please write, and if you could send pictures…

Thank you so much.

Love ya,
Mom and *Dad* White

* * *

Dear daughter and family,

I don't know what we are going to do. We are now selling in our home in St. Johns and the one in Snowflake, Arizona.

Dad looks awful, so wrinkled and old-looking, and so thin; life has not been good to him either. We have decided to sell everything and let God take us home.

Honey, sometimes we do not realize that we make our childhood what it was. I am now writing about mine, how I was locked up in closets and beaten with paddles with holes in them. How my mother let one of her men friends hold a gun to my head and threaten to kill me if I didn't do what I was told. I am not sure that I made my childhood what it was. I am trying to decide why I was beaten with whips, and willow limbs, and so many awful things. I am writing on child abuse in the home. I am learning a lot of why I was that way I was when you children were growing up. It takes a lot of painful years to even to start to understand why we things, and even then, we do not always understand. I was a baby raising babies, and I am not making excuses for myself.

You and Jr. were the ones who were the good ones and always tried so hard to do what was right. JR was my firstborn, and there is not a day that does not go by that I do not think about him, and when I do, I shed many tears. Just like when I think about you. I cry a lot, as I do miss you so much; even as I type this, the tears fall. I love you so, and I remember each one of them. I hope you do also, the times we would go to Catalina Island and so many different places. I always wanted you to have everything. I guess

I didn't know how to show you the love you wanted, although I did my best I knew how.

If Dad had been home and not on the road all the time, it would have been different also. I am not blaming Dad either, as he was doing the best that he knew how also. Dad and I have always wanted the best for all of you. You have done well with your life, and we like to know our son-in-law before it is too late.

It will not be long before Dad and I will not be around very much longer. I can see the pain in Dad's face, and how aged he has become. You would not recognize him on the street.

I try to keep in touch with Donna; however, I did not know that Mark was getting another divorce. Mark, I don't believe, will ever grow up.

Well, honey, I wanted you to know that I love you and so does dad. And that we love your family, so please let them know. Love you.

Mom and Dad

* * *

Dear daughter and family,

Just had to write to you to let you know it won't be long now 'til we have most things sold. Then we will no longer be here.

Honey, I want you to know that we love you and miss you.

I love you and hope you can forgive me for our disagreements. My life is so different now. In fact, you would not recognize me inside and out.

There should be a manual for young mothers that come with their babies. I started raising babies, and I really was only a child myself. Please forgive me for all of my mistakes. I have learned so much that I didn't know about myself. I am writing a book on child abuse. Hoping it will help others. All I can do is ask for your forgiveness and pray that you will come and see me.

Dad and I would also like to know our son-in-law. We know he is a good person and loves you and the boys. I want to thank him for that. I hope that he will let us.

Cris, thank you for the precious daughter you are and for all the wonderful memories that I carry with me.

Honey, I want you to know that I was never angry with you, ever.

I love you more than life itself and always wanted you to be a happy princess and to marry a wonderful prince. I realize now that you have found your prince, and he is your choice. Parents want the best for their children (as you know now). I am very proud of you. Just want you to know that you made a wonderful choice for a husband. I want him to know that I love him also, and so does your dad.

Honey, yes, things can be done differently. Our love can flow forward for each other. God says in his wisdom word that situations do change, and so do people. Nothing ever stays the same. Love can flow. (God says nothing is impossible.) Please, please forgive me. There is so much to tell you and to ask for forgiveness, and I hope your husband can forgive me also. You, both, as one. So it is him also I must ask for forgiveness.

I have become very humble. God has been showing me the way through his Word. I am no longer the young person I was. I guess God gives us much wisdom as we grow older. I wish I had it in my youth as I was raising my children.

Thank you, daughter, for who you were and who you are. If I could have more children, I would want them all to be like you. You are both beautiful, inside and out. You were and still are so perfect to me. Just wanted you to know that. There is never a day that doesn't go by that I do not think about you or look at your picture.

God be with you and your family. God knows how much you mean to me, and I so want to know your husband. We love all of you. Thank you again, daughter, for you and your family.

Must go for now. Give your precious boys and husband a hug for us. Honey, I am really sincere and want you to know that.

There are somethings I cannot tell you in a letter.

Love you always,
Mom and Dad for always

* * *

Dearest Daughter Crystal and family,

So far, we still have Dad with us. He was almost killed last month. I took pictures of the wreck, and he has had a concussion. He seems to be better now, however, he still does not act the same sometimes.

The news that I have to tell you cannot be put into a letter and must be told to you in person. I just hope that we, Dad and myself, are still around to tell you. It is really important that you know, or I wouldn't be putting so much about it.

I also want you to know that we are going to be moving far away from here and don't know when we will ever see you again once we move. (This is not what I was going to tell you. This I can write down on paper.) Dad and I are selling everything that we own and moving back into a fifth-wheel trailer. If there is anything that you want to get, you need to do that now, as I am having the auctioneers sell everything, except for a few clothes on outback. Time is short for both Dad and myself, so we are doing away with everything; that way, there won't be any problems with stuff to get rid of when we leave this earth.

We don't want to burden you children with anything, and we are trying to get everything into order before God takes us home with Him.

Please don't feel that you need to see us. We want you to see us because you love us. I am not writing this letter to you so that you will see us. I am just letting you know that we are now getting ready to put our life together so that when we leave this home here on earth, we do not put our burdens onto anyone else. Please try to under-stand what I am saying, and please know that we both love you very much and always will, and that you will always be in our hearts no matter what.

You take care and let your family know that we love them also.

Sending you all our love,
Mom and Dad

ABOUT THE AUTHOR

Crystal White resides in Wyoming. She enjoys spending quality time with her partner, friend, and loving husband, Daniel. After, Shawn passing away to join Jesus Christ, Crystal's heart broke and feeling lost without Shawn. Their marriage of thirty–two years, with memories of happiness and sadness was unbareable, until, Crystal and Daniel found that their paths crossed together. Daniel also lost his loving wife into the heavens. Daniel and Crystal bonded as friends. The plans of *God* brought a wonderful union between both families. Crystal's sons and Daniel's daughter are anchored into a loving and beautiful relationship.

CPSIA information can be obtained
at www.ICGtesting.com
Printed in the USA
FSHW021951280620
71530FS

9 781645 442264